Reason for Leaving

Reason for Leaving

JOB STORIES

A Novel

JOHN MANDERINO

Published in 2001 by
Academy Chicago Publishers
363 West Erie Street
Chicago, Illinois 60610

Printed and bound in the U.S.A.

Library of Congress Cataloging-in-Publication Data

Manderino, John.
    Reason for leaving : job stories : a novel / by John Manderino.
        p. cm.
    ISBN 0-89733-499-X
        1. Separation (Psychology)—Fiction. 2. Job satisfaction—Fiction. 3.
Occupations—Fiction. 4. Young men—Fiction. I. Title.

PS3563.A46387 R43 2001
813'.54—dc21   2001053481

To Linda,
in loving memory

☆

Delivery Boy

So. How are you doing, young man?

Fine, Mr. Novak.

Here. Shake my hand. I'm seventy-eight years old. How do you like that grip?

It hurts.

Does it?

Yes!

Does it?

Please!

Please is good. Would you like a piece of coffee cake?

No.

I'll cut you some. It has cinnamon. Do you like cinnamon?

It's all right.

Here. Eat that. What do you say?

Thank you.

What grade are you in?

Seventh.

How much is eight times four?

I don't know.

Thirty-two. Do you have a girlfriend?

No.

Don't you like girls?

They're okay.

How's the coffee cake?

Fine.

I'm seventy-eight years old.

I know.

Mr. Novak is from Poland and looks like Lawrence Welk. He's the owner of Novak's Meat Market, where my dad's a butcher. My dad's been working there since he was fourteen and still calls him Mr. Novak. So do the other two butchers, Bob Stanwyck and Hank the German. So do all the customers. Uncle Bobby says Mr. Novak's *wife* probably calls him Mr. Novak.

Uncle Bobby's my mom's kid brother, my dad's godchild, and my delivery partner every Saturday. He drives and I run the bags of meat up to the door and run back with the money and maybe a dime or a quarter for myself. Uncle Bobby is skinny and swaybacked and wears a snapbrim cap and sunglasses, which he calls "shades." While Mr. Novak looks like he could play polkas on the accordian, ordering everyone to dance whether they want to or not, Uncle Bobby looks like he could play the saxophone, some cool slippery blues—although in the car he plays the country western station. Our favorite song is "The Wabash Cannonball," especially the fingerpicking part.

* * *

"Godfather!" Uncle Bobby shouts as we walk in the shop at seven in the morning.

"Godchild!" my dad shouts back, and stops cutting up whatever he's cutting up.

They talk about how they bowled Wednesday night while I find a chair, close my eyes and pretend I'm back in bed where I belong.

I fall asleep.

I dream that Lucille Hanratty comes up to me after school and says she likes me. This makes me very happy. But she wants to shake my hand and I don't want to because I know she'll turn into Mr. Novak. "Don't you like me?" she says, holding out her hand . . .

"Hey. Moonface. Let's go," my dad tells me, and I wake up and follow him and Uncle Bobby into the freezer to begin lugging bags of meat out to the car, each bag with a customer's name pencilled across:

Stark

Levin

Petrovitch

Dart

Cohen

Nudo

O'Connor . . .

When the car is packed with bags, with just enough room for us, Uncle Bobby starts the engine and shouts, "We're off like a herd of turtles!"

To Mrs. Stark.

I hate going there.

In the foyer I press the black button beside her name and wait for her suspicious little voice to come out of the speaker box:

"Who is it?"

"Novak's."

"Who?"

"Novak's. Your meat."

A long pause while she decides whether to believe me.

Then the buzzer, and I shove open the door and head up the carpeted stairs.

"Up heeere!" she calls down from the third floor.

How does she get up there?

Maybe she never comes down.

She's in the doorway, tiny, with a papery face and blueish hands, her skull showing through her wispy white hair, and she's all wrapped up in a quilted housecoat in the middle of June, telling me to come in, come in. "Put it over there, on the counter top. I'll go get your check. Please don't touch anything," she adds, shuffling off in her furry slippers.

It's so hot in here.

On the table there's half a cup of tea, the used tea bag on the saucer, a half-eaten piece of toast, a knife with crumbs in a smear of butter, and Doris Day on the radio:

When I was just a little girl, I asked my mother . . .

"Here you are," she says, returning with the check. "And something for yourself." She shows me the nickel, then places it in my palm, and with her cold bony hand closes my fingers over it, an apology in her smile. Sorry it's only a nickel? Sorry she's so old and spooky?

I thank her and get out of there.

Will I be pretty, will I be rich . . .

I take the stairs two at a time and escape into the morning sunlight. I race to the car and Uncle Bobby, who's in there singing along with Buck Owens and the Buckaroos:

I've got a tiger by the tail, it's plain to see,
And I won't be much when she gets through with me . . .

* * *

Mrs. Levin, looking straight at my big Italian nose, says, "You must be Johnny's boy."

She's good for a quarter, though.

* * *

Mrs. Stolowski has to take out every single package and open it and smell it. Then she has to check everything against the bill. Then she has to wash her hands. Then she has to go find her purse.

No tip.

* * *

The Cohen's apartment has a shiny wood floor, throw rugs, books and magazines all around, a painting on the wall that's just a bunch of lines, and a little weiner dog they call Prince Hal who tries to untie my shoe with his teeth. Mr. Cohen has a beard and sandals, like a beatnik, and Mrs. Cohen looks like a fortune teller. They're very relaxed. I have a feeling they don't believe in God.

Fifty cents, though.

* * *

Garlic-smelling Mr. Petrovitch holds out two fat fists and tells me to guess which one has the silver dollar. Every week, whichever hand I guess, he turns it over, opens it, and it's empty.

"Sorry!" he says with a big laugh.

He never shows me if there's a coin in the other hand.

* * *

The Darts have a daughter a little older than me. I don't know her name. She comes to the door half-asleep in a house-coat she holds at the throat, her hair every whichway and one eye stuck closed. She's beautiful. I can smell her sleepi-ness. "Here," she says, and hands me a check and closes the door in my face.

I stand there staring at the door.

One day I ring the bell again, but then run.

* * *

Freddy Nudo has the meat brought to his bar, Nudo's Tap.

"How's your old man?"

"Fine."

"Tell him gimme a call. I got a horse for him."

"All right."

"Gonna be a butcher like your dad?"

"No."

"Brain surgeon?"

"Ballplayer."

"Your dad was a damn good ballplayer."

"I know."

"He tell you that?"

"Yes."

"Tell him Freddy said he's full a shit."

"All right."

"So who ya gonna play for? White Sox?"

"I guess."

"Here's a buck, case you don't make it."

"Thank you."

"Tell him to call me."

"All right."

* * *

Heading back after the morning run, we pass a wedding at the church near 90th and Jeffrey, the bride and groom in front of the doors getting their picture taken. Uncle Bobby shouts out his window, "Fools! Fools!"

We laugh like hell.

* * *

Mr. Novak is waiting for me with his handshake and his coffee cake with cinnamon. I understand why he likes to show me he can break my fingers even though he's seventy-eight years old, but I wish he didn't have to show me every week.

My dad fixes me and Uncle Bobby each a couple of ham sandwiches on a paper plate with a big wet pickle. Uncle Bobby reads the *Sun-Times* with his sandwich and I watch my father working.

Under his apron he wears a white shirt and tie, his hair is neatly combed with Vaseline Petroleum Jelly, and he moves around quickly. I like watching him cut meat, slicing along invisible dotted lines that divide the hunk into separate pieces that have names. He's a very good butcher.

But so are Bob Stanwyck and Hank the German. Yet a lot of times they'll go to serve a customer and the person will say, "That's all right, I'll wait for Johnny," like this was a barber shop. The reason is, my dad is such a nice guy he makes people feel good. It's as simple as that. He kids around with them and listens and shares tips on horses or talks about the White Sox, and they can tell it's got nothing to do with trying to sell more meat.

He comes backing out of the freezer with a long tray of pork chops.

"Dad, Freddy Nudo said to call him. He's got a horse."
"All right."
"He told me to say you're full of...you know."
"Shit?"
"Yeah."
"He give you anything?"
"A dollar."
"That's all right, then."

* * *

The afternoon run takes us all the way up by the lake, flying along the Outer Drive, sailboats and gulls out there, ahead of us the Chicago skyline, and Mr. Johnson waiting in his tenth floor apartment, in his red robe, looking down on the Lake and the boats and our little car bringing him his meat.

He invites me in to show me again the photo of him and Mayor Daley.

I tell him, "Nice."

Then the baseball signed by Luke Appling.

"Nice."

Then his World War II sharpshooter medal.

"Nice."

Then he gets this nervous look and says, "Would you like to see something *really* special?"

I always tell him I don't have time to see anything else because my uncle is waiting. "Maybe next week," I tell him.

"All right," he says, looking sad now.

He gives me a fifty-cent piece.

Riding down in the elevator I wonder about the special thing he wants me to see. I'm pretty sure it's his wanger, but maybe not.

* * *

On the way to Mrs. Fitzgerald, Uncle Bobby turns off the radio and tells me a joke about an Indian with the world's greatest memory.

"... but *this* time the guy just says to the Indian, 'How.'"

I don't get it, but Uncle Bobby tells it so well it's still
funny and I laugh and laugh.

"That's not it," he says.

"Oh."

"So when the guy says, 'How,' the Indian looks at him
and says: 'Scrambled.'"

I wait.

"That's it."

I laugh and laugh.

Uncle Bobby sighs and turns the radio back on.

We sing:

The news is out all over town
That you've been seen out running 'round . . .

*   *   *

The Toolan sisters, two old ladies, think I'm such a pleasant
boy, so cheerful.

"Like his father," says one, and the other one nods.

But what it is, they're the very last bag and now I'm *free*.
They give me a nickel.

"*Thank* you! Thank you very much! See ya next week!
Goodbye! Goodbye!"

*   *   *

Back at the shop while Uncle Bobby and my dad check the
bills against the money, I count up my tips: four dollars and
seventy-five cents. My dad gives me a quarter to make it
five. Then he wraps some ham and baloney for me to take
home and walks us to the back door.

I feel bad leaving him here.

But in the car "The Wabash Cannonball" comes on and
Uncle Bobby turns it all the way up:

From the great Atlantic Ocean
To the wiiiide Pacific shore . . .

Altar Boy

QUEEN OF APOSTLES CHURCH
RIVERDALE, ILLINOIS 1962

The pay is lousy, a dollar a year around Easter. But I'm not in it for the money. Neither is Ralph.

"Who we got?" he says, hurrying into the dressing room, pulling off his sweater.

"Crowley," I tell him, working on the twenty-three buttons down my cassock.

"A quicky," he says.

"Yep."

Father Crowley can do a high mass in thirty-five minutes, a low one in twenty. The man's amazing.

We get into our surplices, with the big sleeves like wings, and head down a passageway behind the altar that comes out in the sacristy, where Father Crowley's getting into *his* outfit.

"Good morning, Father."

"Morning, boys."

Father Crowley has the hairiest nostrils I've ever seen on a human being.

Me and Ralph get busy, getting the altar candles lit, getting the water and wine cruets filled. Sometimes, like this morning, Father's back is bad and we have to tie his shoes for him, Ralph taking one, me the other.

Then we're all set to go. We stand in the wings, palms pressed together under the chin, waiting for Father to give the word. Sounds like a pretty good crowd out there for a weekday. You can hear them coughing and fidgeting. Then Father says, "All right." And out we go.

Soon as we appear, everyone stands right up.

That's a very cool feeling.

Father goes on up with the chalice and sticks it in the tabernacle for later, then turns around and spreads his arms and says, *"Introibo ad altare Dei."*

And me and Ralph tell him, *"Ad deum qui laetificat am juventutem meam."*

I don't know what we're saying, but God does and that's the important thing. God is what this job's all about.

I know Ralph feels the same way. In fact, he's probably going to be a priest. Jesus appeared to him in a dream and told him he'd make a pretty good one.

I don't know if it's a job I'd want or not. I mean, I think it would be cool doing Mass, and of course hearing Confession:

Bless me, Father, for I have sinned. I committed an impure act with myself.

My son, that's disgusting.

I'm sorry, Father.

Don't ever do that again. You hear me, boy?

Yes, Father.

Now get the hell outa here.

But the thing about being a priest, you can't ever quit. I wouldn't like that. I like being able to quit.

That's what I told Ralph and he agreed but he said he didn't have any choice. He said Jesus picked him and that was that.

I said, "He didn't actually *pick* you. He just said you'd probably make a good one."

Ralph shook his head. "You didn't see His face."

I feel bad for Ralph because I know he'd rather be a Marine, like his dad. I told him he could be a chaplain, but he said they're not allowed to kill, so what would be the point?

We get to the Offertory in about twelve minutes flat. Father holds up the host and Ralph gives the handbell one clean shake, all wrist, and now the bread is the body of Christ. Then Father holds up the chalice and Ralph rings the bell and now the wine is the blood of Christ. Even if you're not a Catholic, you have to admit that's pretty miraculous.

And we do it here every day.

Ralph goes and gets the paten—the silver plate with a handle, to catch any crumbs—and Father Crowley gives us Communion. Then, with the body of Christ still melting in my mouth, I follow Father down to the railing and go along holding the paten under everyone's chin while they shut their eyes and stick out their jittery tongue. Sometimes there's a kid you know and you're tempted to give him a friendly little stab in the Adam's apple with the edge of the paten. But you don't.

After Communion it's just a matter of wrapping up. Then Father tells them, *"Requiescat in pace"*—Go in peace—and we head back into the sacristy.

"Well done, fellas," Father tells us.

That's what you like to hear. Because if Father is pleased, then God is pleased. And if God is pleased, then you're all set.

I know Ralph feels the same way.

"Semper fidelis," he always says to me when he leaves, meaning "Always faithful." Only, that's not from the Church, it's from the Marines.

Window Washer

CALUMET CLEANERS
RIVERDALE, ILLINOIS 1963

I can't decide whether Lucille Hanratty, if she happened to walk by, would think I look cool doing this or not.

I'm out on the sidewalk washing the big front window of the Calumet Cleaners, where my mother works mornings. It's February, after school, turning dark, and so cold the steaming water I splash onto the window with a long-handled brush turns to ice unless I'm quick with the squeegee. But I don't want to move *too* quickly. I want to appear detatched from this window washing, as I'm detatched from the weather in my unzipped ski jacket, no hat or gloves.

"Missed a spot."

It's Tim Baker. He spits a hocker on the window and points to it: "Right there."

He's with Bob Wilson, who's laughing his fat ass off.

These are my friends.

I say to Baker, "Jag-off," but in a detatched way, and run the wet brush over the hocker. I don't want any trouble. This is my first day on the job, first half hour in fact. And

25

Baker is big, with red hair.

He says, "What'd you call me?" Being with Wilson, a witness, he can't let it go.

I can't let it go either, with Wilson there. "You heard me," I tell him, working away. That's a good answer because I'm not calling him a jag-off again, but I'm not backing down either.

He steps up to me and puts it this way: "Did you call me a jag-off?"

Now the answer has to be yes or no, and with Wilson it has to be yes.

I nod my head.

He nods too, while deciding what to do with me. He decides to reach down and pour the bucket of water over my shoes.

Wilson says, "Whoa!" with a big happy laugh.

Baker sets the bucket back down and stands there waiting for my response.

Even if Wilson wasn't there, I would have no choice. I sigh, swing my fist and catch Baker on the side of the jaw.

"Whoa!" from Wilson again.

Baker steps back and works his tongue around in there, looking at me. He seems pleased. Then he begins a little humming sound, which rises higher and higher, and then he attacks in a blur of wild punches to the head and I go down with blood in my mouth and ringing in my ears. There are also tears in my eyes but I hope he understands you can't describe that as crying. I hope Wilson understands that, too.

They walk away and I get up. Big fat nice Mrs. Petrocelli comes hurrying out, wanting to know what happened.

I tell her some jerk spit on the window.

She tells me I shouldn't take this job so seriously.

In the john rinsing off the blood, I can see in the mirror my lip is already starting to swell. Lucille Hanratty might be drawn to a guy who lives like this, out on the edge, taking shit from no one. I let a trickle of blood run down my chin: *I'm no damn good, Lucille. Can't you understand? I'm trouble, baby. Stay away. Go on home, little girl . . .*

Mrs. Petrocelli taps on the door. "Are you all right in there?"

"Yes."

"Would you like me to call your mother?"

"No."

I wipe off my chin and come out and go fetch the bucket. I fill it up again and lug it back outside, zip my jacket all the way up, and finish the damn window.

Ditch Digger

ILLINOIS CENTRAL RAILROAD REPAIR YARD
CHICAGO 1965

"If you could choose any woman in the world to do it to, who would you choose? Take your time," he tells me.

We have a lot of it, about six more hours, with a break in about fifteen minutes, I'd guess. I don't have a watch. Gary does, but he won't tell me the time. He says I think too much about the time and that's why it goes so slow. Yesterday he caught me sneaking a peek at his watch, so now he keeps it in his pocket.

"C'mon. Choose," he says, digging away.

"I'm thinking," I tell him, resting on my shovel.

Possibly Bridget Wyler, in my biology class this last year. Everyone calls her a whore but I like that about her, all that lipstick and eyeliner and those hoopy bracelets on her skinny wrists and the way she arches her back as she sits down.

"Raquel Welch," I tell him, just to give an answer.

"Not a bad choice," he says. "Rather predictable, though. I'll tell you mine and it might surprise you. Beaver's

29

mom, June Cleaver. Go ahead and laugh. It won't bother me at all."

I'm not laughing.

"See, you don't understand," he says. "You chose Raquel Welch. Well, fine. Big tits, long legs. Sure. Why not? But the thing you don't understand, being a virgin—"

"I told you, I'm not a virgin," I say to him, although I am.

"Right. Okay. The thing you don't understand, being an *idiot*—"

"Hey." He's taller than me and at seventeen a year older, but skinny and weak-looking. "Don't be calling me an idiot."

"Why not? Explain to me why I should not call you an idiot. Go ahead. I'd like to hear."

"Because I'll hit you with this shovel, how's that."

"I rest my case."

He says that a lot—"I rest my case"—meaning I just said something that proves his point.

We work for a while.

We're digging a culvert. That's what Mr. Brunowski calls it, meaning a ditch. That's all we're doing all day long at the far end of a large field full of weeds. Mr. Brunowski wants us to dig approximately two feet deep and six feet wide, all the way around the field. This is our third day. We've both been hired for the summer. I have no idea why Mr. Brunowski wants this ditch, this culvert. I have a feeling he just didn't know what else to do with us. I have a feeling if we ever finish it he'll tell us to go back and fill it all in again. I would

ask him about it, but he scares me. When I put it to Gary, he
said the ditch is for "drainage purposes." He doesn't know,
either.

It's hot out here. It's still only morning and already so
hot.

I stop and rest for a while, leaning on my shovel, wiping
my face with my t-shirt. Gary works on, humming to himself, grunting now and then. His half of the ditch is a good
five feet further along than mine.

"All right," I say to him. "Tell me why."

"Why what."

"Why you would choose Beaver's mom."

"June? Because she's so unhappy," he says, working on.

"Beaver's mom?"

"That's right."

"You're talking about the show, *Leave It to Beaver*."

"Right. She's putting up a good front, but if you knew
anything about women—which you don't—you could see
she's very unhappy. Miserable, in fact."

"Okay, why is that."

"Why is she miserable?"

"Yeah."

He stops working, puts one foot up on the blade of the
shovel and wipes his brow with his forearm. "Because she's
sexually frustrated. Ward just doesn't take her there."

Sometimes Gary scares me more than Mr. Brunowski.

"So, is that . . . part of the show?" I ask, wanting to get
this straight. "Is that what you're saying?"

"How do you mean?"

"Beaver's mom being sexually frustrated—is that, like, part of the *script?*"

He gives a laugh. "I kinda doubt it. It's supposed to be a *family* show." He takes out his watch. "Break time. Let's go."

*   *   *

In the lunch room I buy a Sprite from the machine, find a loose newspaper and sit alone at a table in a corner.

Sox shut out the Indians last night, 2-0. Cubs got pulverized by the Pirates, 13-2. I study the box scores. I have a deep desire that a few years from now *my* name will begin appearing there, and a deep fear that it won't.

Gary's at a table with a group of loud relaxed men, acting like he's one of them.

"Yeah, Brunowski's got me out there keeping an eye on the kid," I hear him say.

A little man in a shirt and tie and pens in his pocket walks up to me and introduces himself as Al Russo from Personnel, the guy who got me the job here—as a favor to my dad, he explains.

I want to tell him he had no right to do that. But I thank him.

"So how is it going?" he asks.

"Good. Fine."

"What've they got you doing?"

"Just some . . . excavating, basically."

"Oh?"

"Putting in a culvert."

"A culvert. *Well.*"

"For drainage purposes."

"Of course."

"Isn't it *illegal* to hire someone as a favor to their father?"

"Not at all. Listen, good luck with your culvert."

"Thanks."

"And say hi to your dad."

* * *

So hot out here. The sun like a gong. One cloud. One thin, wispy cloud. I stand there thinking of all the hours ahead . . . all the days . . . all the weeks . . .

I let the shovel drop from my hands.

"I'm quitting."

"Again?"

"I can't do this. I'm sorry. Four hours a day I could handle. I could do four hours. But eight. That's ridiculous. Eight hours a day? Five days a week? I'm sorry."

"Tell Brunowski."

"I will. Don't worry."

"Good, because here he comes."

I look and see someone heading towards us across the field and it can't be anyone else because no one else walks like that—in a crouch, craning his scrawny neck, holding his arms away from his hips—like a huge ugly bird unable to fly.

I grab my shovel and begin digging and don't look up until he gets here.

"Hot enough for ya, Mr. B?" Gary says.

He doesn't answer. He stands there staring at the culvert, at how much further along Gary's half is. He looks at me with disgust. "What the hell you been *doing* out here, beating your meat?"

Gary laughs hard at that.

Mr. Brunowski is waiting for me to answer.

"I guess I'm just . . . not very good at this," I tell him.

"What the hell is there to be *good* at? You're digging a ditch, for Christ sake."

"A culvert," Gary says.

Mr. Brunowski points at him. "Don't be a smartass."

"I wasn't being . . . " Gary says, and stops, his eyes looking moist.

Mr. Brunowski tells me to get my lazy ass in gear or he's going to give me a *spoon* to work with. "A *tea*spoon," he adds, walking off.

When he's far enough away Gary says, "Ever see his wife? She works in Payroll. Jesus, what a beast."

We both laugh, so he says it again, "I mean, a *beast*," and we laugh some more.

I feel like maybe Gary isn't really such a jerk.

"What time is it?" I ask him.

"Now, don't start that," he says, wagging his finger at me.

* * *

Lunch time I buy another Sprite and sit alone at my usual table. In my bag I find an apple and two Saran-wrapped sandwiches: strips of my dad's Italian sausage on hamburger buns, with fried green peppers and lots of mustard.

Gary's over there with his Fellow Workers, telling them about Brunowski's visit:

"Starts trying to give me shit. I told him, 'Hey. You wanna play tough-guy with the kid, go ahead. But don't try it with *me*, pal, or I'll put this shovel where the sun don't shine.'"

* * *

It's gotten even hotter out here, and muggy. I feel like the heat is so thick, Time can barely make it through. It has to crawl, slowly, one minute per hour.

I do a lot of leaning on my shovel, keeping an eye out for Brunowski. Gary works away, telling me about a James Bond movie he saw, giving me every scene, even bits of dialogue, and what each of the women looked like.

"And I mean, you should *see* this bitch," he says, and gives a pretty good description, I have to admit. He uses the word "voluptuous."

When he finishes telling me the movie, he says the reason he enjoys James Bond films so much is because he relates to the main character.

"To James Bond, you mean?"

"In many, many ways."

That breaks me up.

"You find that amusing?"

I can only nod my head. Gary and James Bond. I like that.

"Keep it up," he tells me, walking over, shovel raised. "Keep laughing. Go ahead."

"All done," I tell him.

He stands there holding up the shovel, breathing hard through his nose.

"All through," I repeat.

He stands there another moment, making sure. Then he nods. "I rest my case," he says, and goes back to work.

*   *   *

In the lunch room during afternoon break I hear him telling the men at his table, "Brunowski oughta fire that kid. All day, all he does, stand around bitching and moaning like a goddam woman . . . "

A couple of the men look over my way.

"It's either too hot," Gary says in a whiny voice that's supposed to be me, "or the day is too long . . ."

More men are looking.

"Or the work is too hard . . ."

Now they're all looking.

"I'm so sick a this kid, you can't imagine. I finally told him, I said, 'Listen, you lazy little . . .'"

I don't hear the rest because I'm out the door.

To hell with this place. I'm a future professional *ball*player, for Christ sake. I don't need this bullshit.

In the locker room I snatch my shirt off the hook—then stand there with it, trying to think what I'll tell my dad. I sit on the bench, trying to think . . .

* * *

So hot out here.

Gary, digging away, is telling me his theory of the Kennedy assassination. It's very complicated. Jackie masterminded the whole thing.

I look up at that one flimsy cloud, still there. I look down at the shovel in my hands. There's no escape, I realize. And I give up. I surrender to this place. To the sun. To eight hours a day. To work.

I stab the shovel at the ground and stomp it in with my heel, then work the handle back and forth, bring up a load of dirt and weeds, and dump it off to the side. I stab the shovel at the ground again . . .

After a while I notice how hard I'm working. After a while more, I don't even notice that.

* * *

"Okay," Gary announces. "That's it. We're outa here."

My t-shirt is drenched, my back hurts and my legs are wobbly. But I feel pretty good.

We head across the field towards the tool shack, Gary winding up his assassination-conspiracy theory: "So ya see, *that's* the reason she always wore those pillbox hats."

Instead of dragging the shovel behind me, I carry it over my shoulder.

Ballplayer

It's dark when the train pulls into Louisville. I have the little
overhead light on, reading a *Baseball Digest* article on Cleveland Indians manager Birdie Tebbets.

"Excuse me, is this seat taken?"

"No," I tell her. "Not at all."

She's tall, not too homely, a lot older, maybe thirty, in a
bulky sweater and a woolly skirt. Sitting down, she smells
nice, like a vanilla wafer.

Just do your best, I tell myself.

I give her time to set her purse on the floor, turn on her
overhead light, get comfortable. Then before she can open
her magazine, I ask, "From Louisville?"

"I'm sorry?"

"Are you from Louisville. I noticed you boarded here
and I was wondering if you're actually *from* Louisville or
perhaps only visiting. I'm from the Chicago area myself—
the Windy City, as they say." I give a little laugh. "Actually,

it's probably no windier there than, well, Louisville, for example."

"You've been to Louisville?"

"Great city. Wonderful people. My name's Max, by the
way." I can always tell her my real name later, if things work
out.

Her name is Audrey, she says, and I have no reason to
doubt it.

"So," I continue, "you're from Lousiville."

"Actually, no. I was there for a teacher's conference."

"*Well.* A teacher. What is it you teach, Audrey? If you
don't mind my asking."

"Not at all. American history."

"No kidding. I'm kind of a history buff myself."

"Oh? What particular—"

"*So,* where ya headed, Audrey?"

"Atlanta."

"I could tell."

"Really? How?"

"That Georgia drawl. Cut it with a knife."

"Actually, I've only lived there a year. I'm from
Dubuque."

"Hey, great city."

"You've been there?"

"Just passing through. Had a pizza there. Wasn't bad."

"So where are *you* headed, Max?"

Max.

"Actually, I'm on my way to Florida. West Palm Beach.
Baseball tryout camp down there."

"Baseball," she says. "Bet you'll have fun."

I give a laugh. "It's not really for fun, I'm afraid. Good chance of me getting signed right there with a pro club."

"So you want to be a baseball player, huh?"

Like I want to be a fireman or a cowboy.

"It's quite serious," I tell her.

"I can see that."

I'm not getting through here.

"I'd like to sign with the White Sox, naturally, being from Chicago, but what I'll probably end up doing, I'll probably just go with the best offer."

"Good idea." She winks. "Go with the green."

This woman is pissing me off. I look out the window and try to think of a big-league team that's weak at second base. The White Sox, since trading Fox. But another team would sound more believable. I decide on the Cleveland Indians. When I turn back she's reading her magazine.

"Can you keep a secret, Audrey?"

She looks up. "I . . . suppose."

"I haven't told this to anyone, okay?"

"Okay."

"The Indians are after me."

"Beg your pardon?"

"The Indians. They're after me."

"After you?"

"For about a year now."

"Indians?"

"One of their scouts spotted me last spring. They've been hounding me ever since."

"I see . . ."

"Driving me nuts."

"Uh-huh. So . . . what is it they want? Do you know?"

"They want me to *join* 'em, that's what they want."

"I see. Become one of them."

"I told 'em, I said, 'Look—'"

"So you've spoken with them."

"Buncha times. I keep telling 'em, 'Get off my back, will ya? When I make my decision I'll let you know.' Two days later they're calling me again."

"On the telephone?"

"Day and night."

She nods. "And do you ever *see* them?"

"Couple times. One of their scouts ambushed me after school one day."

"But you escaped."

"Eventually."

"And would *I* be able to see them, too?"

"How do you mean?"

"If they were here—one of their scouts, for example. Would *I* be able to see him? And speak with him?"

"I guess. If you wanted. What for, though? I mean, no offense, but I don't think he'd be interested in you."

"Oh? Why not?"

"Well, I mean . . . they don't generally go after women."

"I see. And why is that, do you suppose."

This lady's turning out to be a little strange.

"Well, what could they use a woman *for*?" I say to her.

"She could cook for them, couldn't she?"

"That's . . . true. Except, I think they probably have their own cooks, Audrey. You know?"

"I see. So they're only interested in *you*. Is that it?"

"I'm not saying that. I'm sure they're after other guys, too."

"But they have to be special, don't they."

"Well, they're not gonna go after just *anybody*."

"And what makes you special, Max? Out of all the others."

"Hey, I don't wanna sit here bragging, okay?"

"Just between us."

"All right. Just between us? I'm *better*, that's all. Simple as that."

"Better in what way, Max?"

"A lotta ways, except . . ."

"Yes?"

"I don't have much power."

"I see. You mean like the power of medicine men? Is that the kind of power you're talking about?"

"Not . . . exactly."

I think this woman has a screw loose.

"What kind of power do you mean, Max? I'm curious."

"I'm just saying I wouldn't mind stroking one out now and then, that's all. That's all I'm talking about."

"'Stroking one out'?"

"Just, you know, to see how it feels."

"So you've never . . . 'stroked one out'?" she says, dropping her voice.

"Like I said, I don't have the power. Don't have the *size* really."

"I see. So size is important?"

"For power? Sure. But that's not what they want me for. They already got plenty of power."

"So what *is* it they want you for, Max?"

She's making me nervous, the way she keeps leaning towards me, speaking secretly. Plus the lighting here is spooky.

"*Where* did you say you were going?" I ask, to change the subject.

"Atlanta."

"Hey, great city. Wonderful people. I was there, back in . . . let's see now . . ."

"What do they want from you, Max? Can you tell me?"

"I'm gonna read for a while, okay?"

But she doesn't take the hint. She leans even closer. I can see the veins in her eyeballs.

"Are you afraid, Max?"

"Little bit."

"Afraid they'll hurt you?"

"Who?"

"The Indians."

Oh, man.

"They're not gonna hurt me. Why would they hurt me?"

"So what is it you fear, Max?"

I don't know if she knows it but she has her hand on my knee.

"What are you afraid of?" she whispers.

"Of you," I whisper back.

Her face turns to stone.

She sits back, opens the magazine in her lap and starts flipping through it, looking at the left page, looking at the right.

I think I hurt her feelings.

"Hey," I tell her.

She keeps flipping pages.

"Audrey . . ."

She doesn't look up.

"You didn't scare me," I tell her, "okay? Really. It was just . . . the way you were whispering, that's all. I get a little nervous when people whisper. I'm kind of a nervous person, okay?"

"Well," she says, turning a page, "maybe your Indian friends will help you overcome that."

"Right. Thing is, actually, that was sort of . . . made up. They're not really after me. I was just trying to impress you."

She looks at me. "You thought that would *impress* me?"

"Well, *yeah*. I mean . . . didn't it?"

"Impress me? No. It *alarmed* me, hearing someone say such outlandish things."

"Hey now, wait a minute, it's not *that* outlandish. It *could* be true. Could damn *well* be true, believe me."

"A lot of things *could* be true, Max. It could even be true you once ate a pizza in Dubuque." She returns to her magazine.

Just to show her how much *she* knows, I inform her that my name's not Max.

"I'm not surprised," she says, flipping a page.

God, this woman . . .

I tell her, "You're right. I was never in Dubuque. But I *am* going to a baseball camp and believe me it's not for fun. It's called the Al Haines Baseball School and Tryout Camp and *tons* of pro players got started there, including guys like—"

"Please?" She looks at me in a pleading way. "Do I have to find another seat?"

I don't answer.

She returns to her magazine.

We don't talk anymore after that. She reads her magazine and I rest my head against the window.

A thin bright edge of the moon cuts along, keeping up.

She believed me about the Indians, I know damn well she did. Because it *will* be true. Maybe not with the Indians but it's gonna happen. They're gonna see what I can do down there and they're gonna say, *Sign right here, kid*, because I am one *hell* of a ballplayer and she believed me—and it turned her on. It got her all hot. And she's embarrassed about it now.

Poor old thing.

I fold my arms, close my eyes, and go to sleep.

* * *

On the train ride coming home, the moon is full. Gazing at its woeful face, I think about spending the rest of my life as a train conductor . . . a butcher . . . a businessman . . . a bum, a fucking skid row bum . . .

Gas Station Attendant

LEFTY'S CLARK STATION, SOUTH HOLLAND,
ILLINOIS, SUMMER '67

"And better check the oil," the guy adds.

"The oil?"

"Right."

Up until now I was going good.

I got scared when Lefty—my mother's cousin's brother-in-law or something—said *he'd* go pick up the sandwiches, leaving me alone on my first morning. But I was going good. Guy drove in wanting a fill-up, unleaded. I put the nozzle in the tank, set the trigger, then washed his windshield with the combination sponge and squeegie. Trigger gave a click, meaning the tank was full, but I squeezed in another twenty cents' worth. Came to four dollars, sixty cents. He handed me a five. I hit the little dime handle on my change-maker, which goes *ching-ching*, and the nickel handle and the quarter. "Here you go," I told him. "And have yourself a real good day."

Then I did two women at once. Got them both back on the road real quick and smooth and satisfied.

I like the way the change-maker feels on my belt and I like my blue shirt with the orange *Clark* patch above the pocket.

Then this jerk wanting his goddam oil checked.

After doing his gas and windshield, I open the hood and stand behind it for a minute, close it and walk up to his window.

"Looks pretty good."

"You're kidding. Figured I was down at least a quart."

"Actually, you're not. Looked like she *might* be down, but then . . . she wasn't."

"Pretty dirty?"

"Excuse me?"

"The oil. Is it dirty?"

"Well, little bit, little bit dirty, sure. That's to be expected. But not too dirty, not where you need to have it . . . you know . . . cleaned."

"*Cleaned?* What the hell you talking about?"

"Just saying, that's all."

"Saying what?"

"Just . . . that it's okay, everything's fine, looking good. Prob'ly wanna have it checked again real soon, though. Okay, so that's five on the gas."

"Here."

"Thank you, sir. And have yourself a real good day."

*   *   *

Over our sandwiches at his desk I confess to Lefty I don't know how to check the oil.

He stops midbite. "You're shittin' me."

I backpedal. "What I mean is, I know how to *check* it. I know *that*. I'm just not real sure about the specifics of it, that's all."

"You mean like how to do it?"

"Well . . . yeah."

Lefty takes a long drink of his Coke and releases a long low belch. "You know *anything* about cars?"

"To be honest? Probably not as much as I should."

"Know how to *drive* one?"

"Actually, no, I don't. To be honest."

He nods.

I can tell he's wondering what else I don't know how to do. Like make change. Or dress myself.

* * *

The next guy who wants his oil checked, I call Lefty over, like he told me to, and he shows me all about the dipstick, then has me do it.

"I'd say . . . down a quart, right?"

"Tell him."

I go over to the window and tell the guy, "You need a quart, pal."

"All right."

I return to Lefty. "He said all right."

"All right what?"

"Just all right."

Lefty sighs and goes over to the window.

I slide the dipstick back into its holster. I remember Tim Baker once calling me a fucking dipstick, years ago. I figured it was just a variation on dipshit. But *this* is what he meant. Interesting.

Lefty shows me where to pour the oil, using a funnel. It comes out thick and silky-looking. When I spill some he tells me it's all right, take it easy, not to worry.

But I feel him thinking, You fucking dipstick.

* * *

It's afternoon before I get anyone else wanting their oil checked—a woman in a scarf and sunglasses, like Jackie Kennedy.

When I show her the dipstick she lowers her sunglasses for a better look.

"See right there?" I say to her. "Where the oil stops? Means you're down two whole quarts."

"Oh, my."

"Yeah, you gotta watch that. Don't wanna be driving without oil. Do some serious *internal* damage to your engine."

"I see. Well, thank you. That's very helpful."

"Hey, it's what I'm here for. So. Two quarts?"

"Please."

I have a feeling this woman finds me damned attractive: a young man who knows what he's doing. And I probably don't look too bad either, in my Clark shirt with the sleeves rolled up, the change-maker riding my hip.

After I get her all set and she pays, I tell her, "Don't forget what I said, now."

"Sorry?"

"About your *oil*."

"Right."

"And ma'am?"

"Yes?"

"One more thing."

"What is it."

"You have yourself a real good day."

She drives off.

Standing there watching her go, wiping my hands on a rag, I've got a feeling she'll be wanting that oil of hers checked again real soon.

*   *   *

Before the afternoon is up, Lefty shows me one other thing: how to put air in a tire.

So now I can do it all. Anyone who drives in, I can serve them. I can pump their gas, clean their windshield, check their oil, *give* them oil, put air in their tires—and do it quickly, efficiently, and in a friendly manner.

Riding home on my bike I'm thinking I need to learn just two more things: how to drive a car and how to make love to a woman. Learn those two things and then I'll be set. I'll be all caught up.

*   *   *

By the end of the summer I've learned how to drive a car.

Busboy

It's only four hours, three evenings a week, but I feel like all the time spent in classes and the dorm and in town flies by in a blur and I'm here again, walking around pushing a large plastic garbage can on wheels, stopping at tables to slide the stuff left on trays into the can: the remains of pizza slices and cheeseburgers, styrofoam coffee cups, little creamer cartons, plastic salad bowls smeared with thousand island dressing, ash trays piled with butts and a brown apple core, ketchup-stained copies of *The Northern Star*, balled-up napkins someone possibly blew their nose in. And there's not always a tray. Then I have to touch the stuff.

After clearing the table I wipe it off, holding my breath because the smell of the rag makes my knees buckle.

But I like the stiff white jacket, the pockets stuck shut with starch. I won't wear the cap, though. I'm sorry.

And I won't do a table until the people have gone. Not any more I won't. Everyone chatting, laughing it up, and

I'm clearing away their garbage, asking them, "You through with this tray?"

"What?"

"You through with this tray?"

"Yeah, take it. Have a ball."

And I hate when someone walking by tosses something into my can, especially if they say, "Here ya go." And I *really* don't appreciate people *spitting* into the can as they pass, with me right there. That's happened more than once.

None of this stuff seems to bother Melissa, though.

She works the same shift, other side of the room, wearing the same white jacket—with the cap. She doesn't have a problem with the cap. Maybe she knows how cute she looks in it.

After six, when the boss leaves, we stop and talk now and then, midpoint of the room, standing there with our garbage cans. Melissa is little, in John Lennon glasses, with a space between her teeth, and two brown braids lying in front like an Indian maiden's. She blows her cigarette smoke out the side of her mouth and tells me to cheer up:

"What're you always so *sad* about?"

"It's just the way my face looks," I explain.

"You're sad about your face?"

"No, I mean—"

"Take a slice of lemon, rub it all over your face twice a day. Clear it up in a week."

"I'm saying it's just the way my face *looks*. I just *look* sad."

"Oh. So you're not really sad?"

"Maybe a little."

"Know what *I'm* sad about? This fucking country."

"What about it?"

"Well, let's see, there's the war, for starters."

"Vietnam?"

"No, the *Trojan* war. Jeez, this guy."

"Well, *I'm* sad about that, too."

"Nah, you're just sad about your zits."

"Right. Okay. I got work to do."

"Wait. Know what's *really* good for acne? Even better than lemons?"

"I'm not interested, okay?"

"Sex."

"Pardon?"

"Sex. Best cure in the world for pimples. I'm serious."

"Yeah, well . . ."

"See any zits on *my* face?"

She gives me a little smile, lifts a braid and waves bye-bye with it.

I stand there.

"Excuse me, folks," she tells a crowded table, "let me get some of this out of your way."

* * *

A couple evenings later, the boss gone, I'm strolling down the middle aisle, dreaming away, when a guy in a booth full of fraternity types yells, "*Two points*," tossing an empty 6-ounce milk carton at my garbage can. It hits the rim and lands on the floor.

I stop.

"Get the rebound!" he tells me. "Hurry! Clock's running out!"

I *could* just pick up the milk carton and drop it in the can. But everyone in the booth will cheer because I got the rebound. So that's out.

I could walk over and tell *him* to pick up the carton.

But I can't imagine him obeying me unless I had a gun, and I don't.

Or I could just leave the milk carton where it is and resume walking, shaking my head with sadness and disgust. This seems the best alternative.

But I've stood there too long. Another little empty carton gets tossed from the booth, a tropical punch carton. This one makes it into the can and a cheer goes up.

Okay. That's it. Now I'm mad. I walk over there. I have no idea what I'm going to say.

They're waiting with eager faces.

I tell them I quit.

"*Happy?*" I add.

They're *very* happy, cheering as I march off.

* * *

"Know what you shoulda done? What *I* woulda done?" says Melissa, who saw it all and followed me into one of the storage rooms behind the kitchen, where I left my coat.

I tell her I'm not interested in what she would have done. I tell her goodbye, good luck.

"No hug?" she says, standing there with her arms open.

"Oh." I set my coat down, walk up, and put my arms around her. I hold her carefully.

"I won't break," she says, wrapping her arms around me.

I hold her close.

She arches her skinny little back.

I hold her tight.

"Can't . . . breathe," she tells me.

I let go. "I'm sorry. God. Listen. Goodbye. Okay?"

She takes my arms and places them around her again.

"Let's see how you kiss," she says, raising her face and closing her eyes.

I turn my head and clear my throat. Then I set my mouth on her soft little mouth, tasting cigarettes. She opens her lips a little, slips her tongue in my mouth and slides it around. I do the same, or similar. I don't know if I'm doing it right and would like to ask but of course I can't just now.

She fumbles at my belt buckle and I step back.

"Don't be scared," she says.

"I'm not," I tell her.

"You *look* scared."

"It's just my face."

We take off our clothes, watching each other.

She leaves her little cap on.

* * *

Afterwards I want us to lie there together and talk about it but she's off me and halfway dressed already.

I start getting dressed, too. "Melissa?"

"Yo."

"Was that . . . I was wondering . . ."

"You were fine. Short but sweet."

"Short in length of *time*, you mean? Or . . . length."

"Time."

"So what's a *good* amount of time, would you say, about?"

"*I* don't know. More than a *minute*, anyway. Listen, I gotta get back. I still work here."

"Well, *wait* a second," I tell her, because that was the most astounding minute of my life so far.

"Toodles," she says.

"Melissa?"

She walks out of the room.

And that does it. I fall in love with her.

So now I have to stay.

Shit.

I finish getting dressed, put the white coat back on, and return to my garbage can.

Clerk

One afternoon at the cash register I see this guy in the art section stuffing a big hardcover textbook under his jacket. He has to pass the register to get out of the store and I don't know what to do. I'm thinking how would I feel, getting caught at something like that. But it's part of my job to stop him. But it's not like this is my career. But the boss is really nice. But what the hell's one book? But it looked like an expensive one. But the guy is pretty big . . .

Meanwhile, he's walking right past the counter and out the door. I wait a few moments, then go running out after him, hoping he's disappeared by now in all the sidewalk traffic. And he has, dammit. Well, at least I tried.

An hour later he's back.

This time he's in the literature section. He's got the *Norton Anthology*, thumbing through it, looking to his left, looking to his right, looking towards me.

I look down at an invoice sheet and yawn.

When I look up again, there goes the *Norton Anthology* under his jacket. And here he comes. But this time he makes a mistake. He walks by whistling a little tune through his teeth. Which pisses me off. I ask Carol, who's taking a phone order, to watch the register for a minute.

"Excuse me, sir," I say behind him out on the sidewalk, but he just keeps walking. I step up beside him. "Excuse me," I repeat, grabbing his arm, which is very muscular and he easily wrenches it free, then takes off running.

I hesitate . . . and give chase.

We're in a movie now. Those are important documents under his jacket. Very exciting music is playing as we race down the sidewalk, people making way for us. I should be holding up a badge.

The suspect breaks across the lawn in front of one of the dorms and barrels down a side street, then doubles back to the University Center parking lot, through the maze of parked cars, and heads down towards the lagoon.

I catch up with him at a little bridge that spans a finger of the lagoon. He's leaning over the rail, catching his breath. Lacking a gun and cuffs, I walk up and lean over the rail beside him.

After a moment he speaks, gravel-voiced and still out of breath: "Use to be . . . able to run . . . for miles." He shakes his head. "Cigarettes."

I don't respond.

"You smoke?" he says.

I nod.

"Gimme one, will ya?"

Guy's got nerve.

I give him a cigarette and of course he doesn't have matches either. Lighting his cigarette and mine, I get a good look at him. He looks like a younger, redhaired version of Geronimo on that poster back at the store, a big seller.

"So," he says, "what was it you wanted?"

"What did I want? You stole a book—*two* books—and I want them back, that's what I want. And I'm also gonna have to take your name in case my boss decides to press charges, which he probably will."

He unzips his jacket, and for a moment I'm thinking, *Oh Jesus*, but he pulls out the *Norton Anthology*.

"You're talking about *this*, right?"

I take it from him. "And an art book. I saw you take a big hardcover book from the art section."

"That's at my old lady's. It's a couple blocks, if you wanna take a walk. Up to you. I don't care. I was going there anyway."

"Yeah, well, I'm not sure that's a good idea," I tell him. I don't trust the guy. And why should I? I already know he's a thief, and he could be something worse. Truth is, he scares me a little. Redheaded Geronimo.

He shrugs. "Like I said, it's up to you, man." He walks away.

"What I'm thinking is," I tell him, following behind, "I'm thinking you should come along with me back to the store."

"What for?" he says, walking.

"So I can . . . you know . . ."

"Turn me in?"

"Well, yeah."

He stops and faces me. "No, see, that's no good. Because I think you're right, I think your boss *will* wanna press charges. And I don't feel like going through all that."

"Well, that's too bad, you know? I mean, the fact remains—"

"Look. You got your book. If you want the other one, c'mon with me. Either way, I gotta use the toilet."

He walks off.

I go with him.

We walk for a while without speaking. I feel awkward. I try to make conversation. "So. You a student?"

"Nah. Just a book lover. How come you didn't chase me for the art book?"

I shrug. "Figured you'd be back."

"You understand the criminal mind—that it?"

"Something like that."

He laughs. "Know who you remind me of? Barney Fife. No offense, man."

We walk on.

"You mad now?" he says.

*   *   *

We go around the back, up a wooden porch and enter a kitchen. "Be right back," he tells me and heads down a hallway, unbuckling his pants. I wait in the kitchen, which is surprisingly clean. There's even a bowl of fruit on the table.

After a few minutes of pacing I begin to worry that he snuck out the front. But then I hear the toilet flush.

He returns with the art book. "Lookit this," he says. "Check this out." He lays the book on the table, open to a painting by Dali, the one with the melting clocks. "Tell me this guy didn't do acid. Go on, tell me."

"Dali, yeah."

"Who?"

"Salvadore Dali. Listen, I have to use your phone. I need to call my boss, let him know where I went. And I'm gonna need your name."

"Hey, leave me out a this."

"I'm afraid I can't do that, sir."

"Sure you can."

"I need your name, please."

"I'll tell you what you need, Barney. You need to get the hell away from that phone or I'm gonna hit you. Okay?"

"Okay."

"Sit down, man."

"I should go."

"Sit."

"My boss'll be wondering—"

"*Sit.*"

I sit.

"I'm gonna have a beer," he says. "You want one?"

"No."

"Drink a beer, Barney."

He brings out two cans of Budweiser, hands me one and sits across the table from me, pops opens his can and waits

for me to open mine. When I do, he says, "Here's to friend-
ship," and drinks.

"Let me at least just call the store and tell my boss what
happened. I'll tell him I chased you but you got away."

"So why the hell you been gone so long?"

"I twisted my ankle. That's how you got away."

"So where you calling from?"

"I don't know, a house near where I hurt my ankle,
somebody's house."

"'So are you coming *back*?' he'll say. And what're you
gonna tell him then, Barn?"

"Well, I'd *like* to tell him, 'Yes, I am. I'll be there shortly.'"

"But what about your ankle?"

"It's not that bad. I can walk. It hurts, but I can get
around."

"What're you gonna do, fake a limp?"

"It's not that difficult."

"As long as you don't forget which ankle and start limping around on the wrong one and somebody notices. Then
you're *really* in the shit pit."

"I'll be careful."

He shakes his head. "Nah. See, you don't wanna get
into all that, all those lies. Listen. I used to be just like you.
Then you know what happened? You wanna hear what happened, Barney?"

"My name's not Barney, okay?"

"I'll tell you what happened, Barn. And this is God's
own truth. I killed a man."

I start breathing hard.

"You all right?"

I nod.

"Drink some beer."

I take a drink.

"Anyway," he continues, "*then*, to make it worse, I lied about it. I said I *didn't* kill him. And now, you know how I feel?"

"Bad?"

"Real bad. I feel like . . . well, like a big *liar*. And that's a real lousy feeling, Barn, y'know? Go around feeling like that? I'm telling you this for your own good. You know that, don't you?"

I nod.

He takes a drink. Then he looks at me and winks. "Hey, Barn," he says quietly.

"What."

"I didn't really kill anybody. I was just trying to scare you. Did I scare you?"

"Little."

He laughs. "Guess I'm still kind of a liar. My advice to you, don't believe anything I tell you. Not a word." He sips his beer.

"So . . . were you lying just now?" I ask.

"About what?"

"About not killing anyone."

He sadly shakes his head. "I'll tell you what it is. You get to where you don't even know the truth any more yourself. That's what I'm trying to say. That's what I'm trying to warn you against."

He takes a long drink.

I take one too.

"You've got a lot to learn, Barn. I mean about Life. You know about books. But, see, that's different."

"Can I go now?" I ask. "I'd like to go now."

He shakes his head, no. "Sorry."

"Well, what if . . . I left anyway?"

"I'd have to stop you, Barn. You know that, don't you? So I hope you don't try. Besides, I think we're getting along pretty good here. I think we're becoming pretty good buddies. I mean, sure, we have our differences—you say tomato, I say tomahto, that kind of thing. But basically I think we're on the same wavelength, Barn. And I think you feel it, too."

I hear someone walk up the porch. We both look. A woman in a long black dress walks in, carrying a raincoat.

"*There's* my baby," he says.

"Hey, Jack," she answers, giving him a little smile as she pulls from the raincoat a pair of tall silver candlestick holders. She sets them on the countertop with the coat and walks over.

All I can do is sit there staring because she is without a doubt the most beautiful woman I have ever seen.

"Babe," he says, "I want you to meet a real good friend of mine. This is Barney. Barney, this is my lady and love-goddess, Marianne."

"Hello, Barney." She smiles at me, holding out a long white slender arm for me to shake her hand, which is long and cool and soft.

"Me and Barn were talking deep stuff here."

"Oh?" she says, getting herself a beer.

She's so willowy and milk-skinned and her hair is long and black and her large dark eyes full of God knows what.

"Barney thinks we oughta bomb Hanoi: *Kill them dinks. Wipe 'em all out.*"

She sits with us, frowning at me.

"I didn't say that," I tell her. "I'm *against* the war. I think we should get out. I'm for peace."

"You're flip-flopping, Barn," Jacks says, and turns to Marianne. "He don't know *what* he wants."

She reaches for his hand on the table. "And what do *you* want, Jack?"

She's like a cat, she's like a snake. I would give anything, *anything* . . .

Reading my thoughts, Jack says to me, "Ain't she somethin'?"

I nod.

He laughs. "Hey, Mar, I think you got an admirer."

She smiles at me.

I try to return the smile, but I would hate to see it. I drink my beer all the way down and ask Jack for another.

"What're you, crippled? Twist your *ankle* or something?" he says with a wink.

As I walk to the refrigerator I realize I could very easily dash out the door and make my escape.

Marianne says, "We should order some Chinese tonight. Do you like Chinese food, Barney?"

I tell her I love Chinese food. I tell her my mother's from China.

"Really? You don't look Oriental."

I return to the table. "She was adopted."

Marianne nods, looking puzzled.

Jack says, "Barney. This is what we were talking about."

"What."

"Lies, Barn. And you're not even making sense."

"He's just trying to make a good impression, Jack," she says. "Don't be so hard on him."

"But he's gotta learn to be himself, Mar. People will like you, Barn, just the way you are. You ever watch Mister Rogers? Or are you too grownup for that? Big bookstore clerk and all."

"You work in a bookstore, Barney? How nice," she says.

"Actually, my name's not Barney," I tell her.

"See how he is, Mar? Now he wants to change his name. Wants us to call him 'Lance.'"

Marianne laughs.

At me.

It hurts. Bad.

I ask her, "How does it feel, Marianne, to have a boyfriend who's a common thief?"

She sighs, looking embarrassed—for me. "That's not a very nice thing to say," she tells me.

And Jack adds quietly, "You're a guest here, Barn. Did you forget?"

They both look very disappointed in me.

I stare down at my beer can. "I'm sorry. I didn't . . . it's just . . . you were laughing at me."

She reaches along the table and puts her long cool soft white hand over mine. "Oh, Barney," she says, her voice full of such warmth and kindness that I can't help it, tears come to my eyes. One of them falls right through the opening in my beer can.

"Jack, look," she says tenderly. "He's crying."

If she wants to treat me like a little child, I don't care. I'll be whatever she wants me to be.

"All right, Barn, cut the crap," Jack tells me. "He's just trying to soften you up, Mar, so he can get in your skivvies."

She asks me, her hand still over mine, "Barney, is that true?"

I can't look at her.

"Is that what you want?"

I nod.

She gives my knuckles a slap. "You little . . . *faker*," she says, and sits back.

Jack laughs, getting up. "That's our Barney!" He heads to the fridge. "Who's ready for another one?"

I raise my hand, drinking down the one I've got.

"Attaboy," says Jack. "How 'bout you, babe?"

"Sure. Whose book is that?" she says, pointing to the art book at the other end of the table. "Is that yours, Barney?"

I look at Jack returning with the beers.

"It was *s'pose* to be a gift," he says. "It was *s'pose* to be a surprise."

"Can I see it?"

He slides it over. "Happy birthday," he says glumly.

"It's not my birthday, Jack," she says, turning pages.

"Not any more," he says, looking at me.

I'll be damned if I'm going to apologize. I drink my beer.

"Oh, look," Marianne says. "Isn't this pretty. I love water lillies."

I lean over to see and she scoots her chair closer to mine and moves the book between us.

"I believe that's by Monet," I tell her.

She checks to see—and clicks her tongue. "Goodness, you really *do* work in a bookstore, don't you."

I shrug, pleased from head to heels.

We drink more beer and look at pictures. Marianne is drawn to the prettier ones. She likes Renoir a lot.

Jack has moved his chair to Marianne's other side and when we come to Dali's melting clocks he tells her, "Barney says the guy was doing acid when he painted that."

Marianne shakes her head. "I can believe it."

"It's called surrealism, that style," I tell her. "A movement that began around the turn of the century."

"Well, listen to *you*," she says. "Barney, that's wonderful."

Jack smiles at me, proudly.

"My favorite painter is Van Gogh," I tell her.

"Van Gogh," she says. "Isn't he the one who cut off his ear?"

"Right. Exactly."

"Why did he do that? Do you know?"

"He was in despair."

"So he cut off his ear?"

"It was over a woman. A beautiful, beautiful woman."

Jacks says, "So why didn't he cut off his pecker?"

"*Ja-ack.* Barney and I are trying to have a discussion."

Jack makes pig noises.

He *is* a pig, and if he'd only go away and leave us alone . . .

I find one of Van Gogh's self-portraits and begin telling Marianne a little bit about his life, which I know from the Kirk Douglas movie.

Jack props his head on his hand, closes his eyes and begins making loud snoring sounds.

She punches his arm without looking.

"He's right," I tell her.

"No. It's very interesting, Barney. You know so much! You must be an art student."

"Actually, I'm a literature major, Marianne." I want to kiss her lovely lips. "Are you a student?" I ask.

"Well, no. We both . . . work. What, um, kind of literature do you like to read, Barney?"

"I like Shakespeare a lot."

"Shakespeare. Well. That *is* impressive."

"'To be or not to be,'" Jacks says to the ceiling.

"Jack," she laughs. "That's not Shakespeare." She looks at me. "Is it?"

"Actually, it is. It's from *Hamlet.*"

She slaps his arm with the back of her hand. "Well, look at *you.*"

He gives an exaggerated smug look.

"Marianne?" I say to her.

"Yes, Barney?"

"I was wondering . . . could I . . . "

"Down the hall on the right," Jack says.

I ignore him. "I was wondering if I could read something to you. A poem. I'd really like to."

"Well, sure, Barney. Is it something you wrote?"

"No, it's by Shakespeare, a sonnet."

"Oh, dear."

"It's really beautiful and I think . . . I really think you'll appreciate it." I look around for the other book. "What'd I do with the *Norton Anthology?*"

"The what?" Jack asks.

"The book you . . . that other book."

Jack fetches it from the countertop. "Here ya go. Gimme some a that Shakespeare. Hit me with it, baby."

"I'm sure it's in here somewhere." While I quickly look through the index, Jack stands behind Marianne's chair massaging her neck and shoulders.

"Mmm," she tells him.

I turn to page 674. "This is one of the sonnets he wrote to a woman. No one knows who. She's called the Dark Lady."

"Black chick?" Jacks asks, massaging away.

"It just means anonymous."

"That feels good," she tells him.

I clear my throat. "Okay. Well. It doesn't have a title. So. Here it is." With all my heart I read:

"'Shall I compare thee to a summer's day?'—"

"Hey, I've heard that," she says.

"It's pretty famous," I admit.

"Let the boy read, Mar."

"I'm sorry. Go ahead, Barney."

I begin again, my face close to the tiny print:

"'Shall I compare thee to a summer's day?/Thou art more lovely and more temperate . . .'"

The further I read, the more passionate I feel, seducing her right in front of Jack, making love to her with my words—and they *are* mine, I *make* them mine as I speak them. By the time I reach the concluding couplet my voice is quaking:

"'So long as men can breathe . . . or eyes can see . . . /So long lives this . . . and this . . . gives life . . . to thee.'"

I look at her.

She's sitting there with her head back, eyes closed, lips parted, while Jack is kissing her lovely white neck and waving bye-bye to me.

I close the *Norton Anthology* and leave it on the table along with the art book.

Out on the sidewalk, I begin limping back to the bookstore.

Graduate Teaching Assistant
NORTHERN ILLINOIS UNIVERSITY 1972

I figure "assistant" means I'll be helping out a professor: making coffee, filing stuff, running after sandwiches, maybe correcting some essays. But after a crash course with a dozen others, I'm given my own class: Freshman Composition, section 7, 9–9:50, M-W-F, room 104. I'm supposed to walk in there and be the teacher.

I walk in. They know I'm the teacher because I'm wearing a tie and closing the door behind me. I look at them sitting there looking at me. I haven't quite closed the door yet.

I tell them I forgot my pen.

Out in the hallway I stand against the wall. *I can't do this. I'm sorry. I can't. I'm sorry . . .*

"Sir?"

This great big pretty-faced girl in a lumberjack shirt and bandanna walks up. "You the teacher?"

"What did you want?"

"Sir, my name is Penny Ledbetter? I registered late and all the other freshman comp sections are closed and I was wondering—"

I tell her to go on in.

"Thank you, sir. I appreciate it." She continues standing there. "Sir, are you all right?"

"I'm fine. I just . . . I forgot . . . something."

"You're sweating very heavily, sir. Did you know that?"

"Warm in this tie."

She opens the door for me. "Coming in?"

I shake my head. "I can't," I tell her. "I'm sorry. They'll have to get someone else. I'm really very sorry."

She closes the door. "Sir, none of my business, okay? But is this your first time teaching? Is that why you're out here?"

I nod.

"Can I give you some advice?" she says.

I nod.

"Walk through that door, sir, like you're stepping out of an airplane. You're a sky diver. It's your first jump. Just step through that door."

"I tried that."

"And?"

"I stepped out here again. Which I obviously couldn't do from an airplane. So the analogy doesn't work."

She points at me. "See? You just taught me something. And you *sounded* like a teacher."

"It's easy out here."

"So what happened when you walked in?"

"Nothing. I told you, I turned around and walked out."

"Say anything?"

"Just . . . that I forgot my pen."

She laughs right out loud, right in my face. "I'm sorry, sir," she says, shaking her head, still laughing. "Your pen . . . that's very . . . "

"Get in the room," I tell her, jerking my thumb at the door. She stops laughing.

"Find a seat. In you go."

"That's good, sir. Keep that attitude."

"Hurry," I tell her.

"Right."

I follow her in and close the door behind me.

* * *

Topic: Something about myself that I would like to change.

Cynthia Olmsted writes that she would like to lose ten more pounds for three reasons, each developed in a separate paragraph: appearance, health, self-esteem.

Kevin Wilson wants to smoke less marijuana because his mind *keeps drifting like a boat with nobody rowing and a gigantic waterfall lying ahead and yet who among us is able to say what tomorrow may bring, kay sera, sera, let's just hope the war ends soon but if you want to know where I stand, that's easy, Hell no I won't go!*

Patricia Klein would like to change the fact that she's too nice a person and lets everyone take advantage of her: *Its always the sweat people of this world who get eaten up because lets face it everyone likes to eat sweats!*

Penny Ledbetter, the big pretty-faced girl from the hallway, would like to be less critical of other people, especially her roommate, and briefly describes three basic flaws in her roommate's character: laziness, pettiness, and arrogance. At the bottom of the paper she's left me a note: *Sir, I would stop pacing around so much and try speaking slower. Otherwise very good job so far.*

Then I come to this, from Philip Norling:

I would like to stop thinking about her. She is so beutiful. When she smiles it is like the sun rising in the morning over a field of gently swaying daffidils. I want to hold her in my arms and say "I love you." I want to take her face in my hands and kiss her forehead and her eyelids and her cheeks and her chin and her lips. I want to slide my hands down around her skinny white throat and close my fingers tighter and tighter, looking straight into her beutiful blue eyes until she is dead. That is one thing I would like to change about myself, I would like to stop thinking about her in that evil way. And if I do not stop thinking about her in that way I am going to kill myself like the Romans. You sit in a tub of hot water and cut open your wrists and fall deeper and deeper asleep until your dead. Did you want paragraphs?

I read it over again. He sounds serious. I don't know what to do. It's almost one in the morning. I could talk to him tomorrow after class—*if it's not too late.* Jesus. I call information and get his dorm-room phone number.

Someone grunts hello, half asleep.

"Philip?"

"No."

"Is Philip Norling there?"

"Sleepin'."

"In his bed?"

"Yeah."

"All right. Never mind. Thank you."

* * *

The next morning taking roll I get a good look at him: skinny, pony-tailed, patchy-bearded, slouched down in an oversized army jacket.

Pretty standard-looking.

I tell the class I've decided to set up individual conferences in my office over the next few days to talk about this first batch of papers, and I schedule him for two-thirty this afternoon, with no one afterwards.

I spend the period working with them on some grammar and punctuation problems running through their papers. I try to pace around less and speak more slowly.

* * *

"Phil. Hi. Come on in. Have a seat."

He sits in the white plastic chair I've set by my desk. Casually as I can, I ask him how he's doing.

"Okay. How're you."

"Not too bad. Getting a little sick of all this rain."

"Know what you mean."

"Okay, let me see . . . if I can find it," I mutter, looking through the pile of papers, like his was no different from anyone's. "Here we go. Well. I gave you a B."

"Okay. Thanks." He puts out his hand for the paper but I hold onto it.

"You ask down here about paragraphing."

"I wasn't sure."

"Well, even with a very short piece like this you could probably—"

"Did you want it longer? You didn't say anything about how long. I could prob'ly talk more at the end there."

"No, actually it seems pretty complete: '. . . and fall deeper and deeper asleep until your dead.' Strong sense of . . . closure there."

"How's the spelling?"

"Fine. There's an 'a' in 'beautiful' and you want the contraction 'you're' instead of the possessive where you say 'until your dead.'"

"I have a real problem with that."

"Any other problems you'd like to talk about, Phil?"

"Well . . . "

"Just feel free."

"Okay. The word 'its'? I can never remember. Which one gets the—whaddayacallit—the apostrophe."

"The contraction. The one that breaks apart into 'it is.'"

"Gotcha. Okay, well, thanks," he says, holding out his hand again for the paper.

I hang on to it. "Before you go, Phil, I really think we need to discuss the content. Don't you?"

"What about it?"

"Phil, you talk about killing a girl, about strangling her, and about killing yourself, cutting your wrists in a bathtub. Do you see how I might feel a little bit . . . concerned here?"

"Yeah, I see what you mean."

"Do you?"

"I see what you're saying. Thing is, though—no offense, okay?—but I would have to say you kind of missed the whole hidden meaning of the thing."

"Help me out, then."

"It's like . . . okay, it's like when Jim Morrison of The Doors, on the album *Strange Days*, where he says, 'What have we done to the earth? Stuck her with knives in the side of the dawn and tied her with fences and dragged her down.' See, that's what *I'm* doing in this paper: speaking . . . you know . . . "

"Metaphorically?"

"Right. Exactly."

"So you're saying the girl is used as . . . "

"A symbol. That's all. Just a symbol."

"Symbol for what?"

"For . . . you know . . . *whatever*. For Life itself."

"Explain."

"Okay, it's like, there's Life, right? Life is wonderful, Life is beautiful, but it can also be a bummer and you'd like to strangle it. That's all. That's all I was trying to say."

"What about cutting open your wrists in a tub of warm water?"

"Same deal. The whole . . . symbolic thing going on there. I shoulda made it a lot clearer, I know, but you didn't give us a whole lotta time. I'm not complaining, I'm just saying. And I think a lot of other people felt the same way. Just telling you what I heard."

"That I didn't give enough time?"

"It was like twenty minutes before we got started—so that's, what, half an hour to write an essay? I mean, you're the teacher, and I don't wanna be telling you how to do your—"

"No, you're right, you're right. I didn't realize—"

"Hey, no big deal. Live and learn. Anyway, I better get going. I got—"

"Phil, listen. I'm going to be honest here. I'm thinking I should show this to my supervisor Dr. Cunningham and let her decide what to do about it, if anything. This is my first teaching job, and actually, even if it wasn't—"

"This is your first teaching job?"

"Right."

"Coulda fooled *me*, man."

"Oh?"

"It's like you been doing this all your life."

"Well, thank you. Actually, after a little initial stage fright, I really began to—"

"See, the problem is, if you give it to your boss? She's gonna read it and think, Whoa, this guy's a sicko, he needs help, blah, blah, blah, and if I try to explain to her, like I did with you, about Jim Morrison and The Doors, she's gonna say, The *who*? and I'm gonna say, No, that's a *different* group, that's Pete *Townshend's* band, and she's gonna say to herself, This guy really *is* a whacko. You see what I'm saying?"

"That's very good, I like that, The Who. But I think you underestimate Dr. Cunningham. First of all, she's a very—"

"I'll bet I know who *you're* into. Bob Dylan, right? You're a Dylan head. Am I right?"

"Guilty as charged."

"I could tell. See, that's why you're able to understand what I was trying to do in my paper—because I mean, let's face it: Dylan, he's the master. Talk about *symbolic*: 'Einstein disguised as Robin Hood with his memories in a trunk passed this way an hour ago—'"

"'—with his friend a jealous monk,'" I cut in. "Yeah. 'Desolation Row.' Great song."

"Great album," he adds.

"*Bringing It All Back Home*, right?"

"No," he corrects. "*Highway 61 Revisited*."

"You sure?"

"I'm sure."

"I'll have to check that."

"Feel free."

"I saw him down in Carbondale last year," I tell him.

"Hey, I was there," he says. "Great concert."

"Think so? I was a little disappointed. Those three girls as backup singers. Seemed a little slick for Dylan."

"I know what you mean. I remember thinking, *What's with the chicks*? But hey, that's Dylan, right? Always changing."

"That's true. That's a good point," I tell him.

"Hey listen," he says, getting up, "it's been cool talking to you. Not many teachers I can really open up to, you know?" He takes the paper out of my hand. "I'll look this over. See where I went wrong. Maybe next time I'll get you some paragraphs."

"There ya go."

"Hey. Dylan forever."

"Right on," I tell him.

"Catch ya next time," he says.

"Okay, man."

When he's gone I tilt back in my chair, feet on the desk, hands folded behind my head, staring at my Dylan poster on the wall . . .

I sit up. For Christ sake, *that's* how he knew.

* * *

He's not in class next time and I'm worried. Afterwards I phone and get his roommate.

He didn't slit his wrists. He swallowed a bottle of barbiturates. His roommate found him on the floor and called the health center.

"So is he okay? Do you know?"

"I guess. They pumped his stomach. He's still over there."

"But he's okay, right? He's gonna be okay?"

"Prob'ly. He didn't take that many. I don't know where he got 'em. They weren't mine. I don't even *do* downers. I just had 'em for sleep. Can I ask who's calling?"

* * *

He's in a room by himself, sitting up in a hospital gown, flipping through a *Rolling Stone* magazine. He looks pale and very tired. But he starts talking right away.

"There's an interview here with Mick Jagger. He talks about Dylan. Says some cool things. Do you like *Let It Bleed*?"

"Do I what?"

"*Let It Bleed*. The Stones album. You like it?"

And that's all he's willing to talk about—music.

At one point I say to him, "Phil . . . "

"I don't wanna discuss it," he says, "okay?"

"Have your parents been informed?"

"Yeah. They're on the way."

"You fooled me, Phil. You know that, don't you? You fooled me."

"How do you mean?"

"I think you know."

"Hey, you like The Dead?"

"Pardon?"

"Grateful Dead. They got a new one out. You heard it?"

* * *

I go to see my supervisor—tiny, white-haired Dr. Cunningham—and tell her about Phil. She listens carefully.

Then she takes off her glasses, sets them on her desk, folds her hands and says, "Let me make sure I understand this correctly. A student in your class turns in a paper in which he talks about wanting to kill himself, and mentions the method he intends to use, then subsequently does in fact try to kill himself—and you're just coming to see me *now*? Is that what you're telling me?"

"Well . . . basically."

"That is appalling."

"Thing is . . . "

"That is utterly inexcusable."

"I understand what you're saying, Dr. Cunningham, I really do, but—"

"What section."

"Sorry?"

"The class. What section number."

"Seven."

"I'll get someone to take over. Your assistantship is terminated."

"Dr. Cunningham, listen . . . "

"Please leave this office. Now."

I don't especially care for her tone of voice and would like to point that out to her but I've got this hard little ball in my throat.

* * *

I'm supposed to conference at one o'clock with that girl Penny Ledbetter. I call her room and catch her just as she's leaving and tell her not to come to my office, to meet me in a booth in the Pow-Wow Room at the student center. I put a note on my office door canceling my other conferences.

Just before she arrives I change her grade from a B+ to an A-, what the hell.

When I give her the paper she asks about the minus.

"I don't know. Listen. I got fired."

"Wow. What for?"

I tell her about it.

When I'm through she sits there shaking her head at me. "Hate to say it, sir, but your boss is right."

"Well, thanks. I appreciate your support."

"You shoulda moved on it right away. Something like that? God. I mean, just think, sir, how you'd feel if—"

"I know, I know," I tell her, pressing my face into my hands.

"Still kind of shitty though, losing your job and all. You were doing pretty good."

I come out from my hands and give my eyes a flick. "You think so?"

"After you quit pacing around so much."

"Right. Thanks for the tip, by the way."

"No problem. Well, I'd better be—"

"Anything else?" I ask.

"Sir?"

"About how I did. Just wondering."

"Well . . . "

"Was I funny? At all? You think?"

"Not at all, sir."

"I mean when I wanted to be. Couple times there I said some rather . . . witty things, I thought."

"I wasn't always paying attention. Listen, I'm gonna go now, so—"

"Well, wait. Let me buy you a cup of coffee."

"No, thank you, sir."

"You don't have to call me 'sir' anymore, Penny."

"That's all right, sir." She gets up.

"What's your hurry?"

"No hurry."

"So what's the problem?"

She shrugs. "I guess I just don't like you very much, sir."

"You don't?"

"But I hope things work out for you. I really do. So long, sir." She walks away.

I sit there, staring after her.

"Excuse me, you through with the cup?"

"What?"

"You through with the cup?" a busboy asks.

"Yeah. Take it."

He drops it in his garbage can.

"Nice hat," I tell him.

Security Guard

ART INSTITUTE OF CHICAGO 1973

I'm in the Impressionist wing today, with Frank. Frank's an old ex-wino who *likes* working here. He strolls up to people in front of a painting, stands next to them with his hands behind his back and reveals some little-known fact about the artist. I don't know where he gets his information. This morning I heard him telling a man that Toulouse Lautrec was afraid of dogs: "Being such a *little* fella, y'see." The man nodded and walked away.

We wear a burgundy jacket with an Art Institute patch on the breast pocket, white shirt, gray tie, gray pants, black shoes, and walk around, and around, and around.

Occasionally someone will come up and ask me something, usually directions. I'm always a lot more obliging than they want me to be. I can't help it. I'm so glad to be doing something. Often I'll even take the person where he's going. He clearly doesn't want me to but I don't care. And if I work here *another* three months I know I'm going to begin sidling up to people and telling them Picasso never liked to wear hats, or Cezanne's great-grandson invented the electric can-opener.

I used to enjoy coming here, as a civilian. The galleries I'm working today were among my favorites. But not any more. I can't *see* any more. I stand in front of a painting and look and look and it's no use. *Gallery white-out*, it's called.

This morning I'm standing in front of Van Gogh's *The Bedroom*, staring hard. I know for a fact I used to like this painting a lot. There was something it did to me. Gave me some kind of feeling. Damned if I can remember.

"Excuse me, where's the men's room?"

"C'mon, I'll show ya."

* * *

Sometimes Frank will stroll on over for a visit, hands behind his back: "All quiet on the western front?"

"So far," I answer.

"That's good. No news is good news."

"There ya go."

He sighs. "I sure as hell wish they would issue us fire-arms."

He complains about this a lot.

"You put your life on the line and they don't even give you the means to defend yourself?" he says, and shakes his head. "It's just not right."

"Nope," I say.

"See that old witch over there by the Renoir?"

"Yeah?"

"Wanted to know why all these paintings are so *blurry*. Were the artists all nearsighted? So I says to her, 'Ma'am, that's the way they painted. They *wanted* it to look like like that. It's called Impressionism, ma'am.' She says, 'Well, *I'm* not impressed.' And you know what she does? You ready for this?"

"Ready."

"She reaches into her purse."

"Huh."

"Right away I'm thinking, *Gun*, right?"

"Right."

"I'm thinking, 'This woman's gonna shoot me dead and there ain't a goddam thing I can do about it.' See what I'm saying?"

"Yep."

"It just ain't right."

"Nope."

We stand there.

"So. Did she?" I ask.

"Did she what."

"Pull out a gun."

"Handkerchief. But what about *next* time?"

"Exactly."

He sighs, "Oh, well."

I nod.

He grabs my arm: "Hey. If we're so smart, how come we ain't rich?"

"There ya go."

"Catch ya later, partner," he tells me, strolling off, hands behind his back.

*   *   *

Giving us guns would be a bad idea.

For example, this guy this morning comes walking by in his beard and tweed jacket, looking at me, holding up his wrist and tapping it. Couldn't say, "What time is it?" That would be showing too much respect.

But what's worse, I immediately push up my sleeve and tell him, "It's just about twenty-three—make that twenty-four—minutes after nine."

He doesn't say thanks or even give a nod but just turns and stands with his back to me in front of Cassatt's *The Child's Bath*.

And you see, at that point I might have pulled out my gun and splashed his brains all over a priceless work of art. A woman of course is worse, especially if she thinks I've been following her around, admiring this or that about her. Then if I come up and stand beside her in front of, say, Seurat's *Sunday on La Grande Jatte* and mention the Pointillist movement, you know what I get? A sigh. Meaning, *Please. You're a security guard. Do you really expect me to talk to you?*

And see, there again, if I had a gun? Who knows?

*   *   *

Anyway, Christ, what a long day.

I'll tell you what helps a lot though: a good solid daydream. I've just a started a new one today.

I play second base for the Tokyo Giants, one of the few Americans in the league. I'm quite popular but I'm a very private person. In fact, during the off-season I live in a Zen Buddhist monastery in Kyoto. As it happens, the abbot there has a brother who's an excellent chef and a big Giants fan and he'd be thrilled to meet me. So it gets arranged and I go to his house for a wonderful shoes-off Japanese dinner—no sushi though. Turns out, the man has a daughter. Her name is Shuko, and oh my God is she gorgeous, just an unbelievably beautiful young woman who, like her father, is also a big Giants fan, so of course this is quite a thrill for her as well—although it's hard to tell, she's so darned quiet and shy.

So there's the set-up. Then it's just a matter of playing it out very slowly, through many details. By lunchtime today Shuko and I haven't even kissed yet, so that's good. There's a downside to daydreaming, though. And that has to do with trying to stop.

If it's a really good one, I'm still at it on the bus ride home and even after I arrive. I'm ashamed to say this, but I sometimes actually spend the evening walking slowly around the apartment, hands behind my back.

Now and then I'll suddenly notice myself and stop in my tracks, aware that I should be doing something better with my life, something more meaningful. But nothing in particular occurs to me. And I walk around some more.

VISTA Volunteer

There's this remarkable little kid in my reading-writing group. His name is Darryl Potter. He's seven, he's black, and I swear if he works really hard he could be another Henry Aaron. I mean it. You should see this kid hit.

He bats righthanded but I'm trying to turn him into a switch-hitter. He's a little resistant, though. I keep explaining the advantage it will give him later on, but he doesn't care about later on, he just wants to have fun. I'm trying to break that attitude, but he's very stubborn. He also has a little temper. When he gets mad he calls me a butthead. Otherwise he addresses me as *Mister* Butthead.

In our staff meeting this morning this girl Peggy asked me about that, about Darryl calling me Mister Butthead.

I explained that a couple weeks ago he started calling me a butthead—just trying out a funny new insult—and I said to him, making light of it, "That's *Mister* Butthead to you." And he took me seriously.

Joel removed his unlit pipe from his mouth. "It's clear the boy doesn't intend any real disrespect. In fact, it may

95

even be a term of genuine affection. Still, he *is* calling you a butthead, 'Mister' or otherwise."

Sarah wanted to know what exactly *is* a butthead, anyway. "I mean, what are you saying about a person when you call him that?"

"Well, *anatomically* speaking," Eric said, "if you have a butt for a head, you obviously don't have a whole lot of brains. In fact you'd have, well, let's face it, shit for brains."

Stan wasn't sure he agreed. He felt the term had less to do with being stupid than with being foolish.

Jeremy said it meant both: "When you call someone a butthead you're saying the person is basically a stupid fool."

Everyone looked over at me, I guess to see how it fit.

I played with my pen.

Miriam finally spoke. She's the executive director here, a handsome black woman in her fifties with beautiful hands and this elegant serenity that bugs me a little. She said the question is simply this: by allowing Darryl to call me a butthead, what kind of message are we sending him and the other children?

So that went around the table for a while.

Conclusion: a bad message.

We moved on to a discussion of upcoming Black Awareness Week.

*   *   *

This afternoon I take Darryl aside after our reading-writing group and squat down on my haunches, put my hands on his shoulders, look him in the eye and tell him, "I don't want you to call me Mister Butthead anymore, Darryl. All right?"

"Why not?"

"Because it sends a message that you think I'm a stupid fool. Is that the message you want to send?"

He nods.

"But what if it hurts my feelings, Darryl?"

He shrugs.

"All right, look. Just don't use it in front of any grownups, okay?"

"Why not?"

"Because it makes me look bad, letting a kid call me a butthead."

"*Mister* Butthead."

"Right. Tell you what. Let's make it simple. Don't call me a butthead or Mister Butthead any more—anywhere, anytime. Otherwise, you and I are all through hitting base-balls." I don't mean it, but how is he to know? "All right? Clear enough?"

Tears appear in his big brown eyes.

So I tell him I'm sorry, I didn't mean it, he can call me anything he likes, and give him a hug.

He locks his arms around my neck.

"Still buddies," I tell him, "right?"

"Would you pitch to me?"

"Not right now. A little later."

"No. Now."

"Darryl . . . "

"Please, Mister Butthead?"

"You're choking me."

"Please?"

"Let go, Darryl. I can't breathe.

"Will you pitch to me?"

"Darryl . . . "

"*Will* you?"

"Yes."

"Right now?"

"Yes!"

He lets go.

Powerful little arms on him.

* * *

We've got a large plastic bucket full of rubber balls and a nice little twenty-eight-inch Louisville Slugger. That's what started it all, when I found the bucket and bat in a closet in the gym. I was with Darryl looking for some stupid action-figure he'd lost. He was all upset about it, so I said let's go hit some balls and we went out behind the Settlement House where I scratched in his strike zone with a stone against the brick wall and started lobbing pitches to him, underhand. He was terrible, missing the ball by a foot. That was a month ago. Now I'm standing forty-five measured feet away, throwing overhand, hard, and he's belting them one after another. The kid's amazing.

Today though, he seems a little unfocused, falling back into some bad habits.

"Darryl, what'd I tell you about your front shoulder?"

"*Throw.*"

"First answer my question."

"What."

"Your front shoulder. Where are you supposed to keep it?"

"Pointed at you."

"All right, then."

I throw . . . and duck just in time.

"*Attaboy,*" I tell him. "Take my head off."

"Your butthead."

"Okay. Now I want you to switch," meaning I want him to bat lefthanded for a while.

"I don't *wanna,*" he says.

"Don't give me a hard time. Let's go. Other side."

"Why can't I just do it this way?"

"I already told you, Darryl. I already explained. Against a right-handed pitcher a lefthanded batter has a much better chance than a righthanded batter, and against a *left*handed pitcher a *right*handed batter—are you listening?"

"Uh-huh."

"The point is, the batter who can hit both ways always has a much better chance. And that's what *you're* gonna have, Darryl."

"Can't I just—"

"Listen. Someday you'll thank me. When that pro scout comes walking up after your high school game and says, 'Darryl, would you please sign your name on this contract?'—you're gonna say to yourself, 'Thank you, Mister Butthead, thank you.' I only wish someone made *me* bat from both sides, Darryl."

I might not be here throwing rubber balls to a seven year old.

"I don't wanna do lefty," he says.

"Okay. Well, I guess we're all through here. Help me round up the balls."

"I'll do lefty."

"Attaboy."

*   *   *

Monday's the beginning of Black Awareness Week. On Friday each of the Settlement House groups will give a little presentation on the gymnasium stage for members of the community. I've got the kids in my reading-writing group doing historical figures. Latisha's going to be George Washington Carver; Allen will be Frederick Douglas; Gregory is W.E.B. Dubois; Jonella is Harriet Tubman; Erica is Rosa Parks; James is Martin Luther King; and I want Darryl to be Jackie Robinson, but he's giving me trouble. He wants to be King.

I tell him after class he can't be King because James is going to be King."

"You said we could choose."

"I know but you can't both be King."

"Let *James* be Jackie Robinson. He don't even care. He *tole* me."

"Darryl, I'm really surprised. I thought you'd *wanna* be Jackie Robinson. You know, if it wasn't for him—"

"I wanna be King."

"Well, you can't. I'm sorry."

"Then I don't wanna be *in* it."

I shrug. "That's up to you."

"You're a ugly butthead."

I sadly shake my head. "And *you* want to be Martin Luther King?"

"You're Martin Luther *Butthead*!" he yells, and runs crying from the room.

* * *

Next morning Miriam wants to see me in her office. She's just had a long conversation over the phone with Darryl's grandmother.

"Why won't you let Darryl be Martin Luther King?"

She's sitting behind her desk with this intense calmness, or this calm intensity. She offered me a chair but I said my back's bothering me. I want the height advantage.

"James Davenport is doing King," I explain.

"According to Darryl, James doesn't care who he plays. So why not—"

"I just think Jackie Robinson would make an excellent role model for Darryl, that's all."

"Whereas King wouldn't?"

"Jackie Robinson would be more appropriate."

"Because?"

"Okay. You're aware that I've been pitching to Darryl in back of the building, right?"

"Yes, and I think it's wonderful."

"I have never seen a kid his age swing a bat the way he does. And he learned it like *that*," snapping my fingers. "He couldn't even make contact with the ball a month ago and now he's like a—like a *machine*."

"A machine."

"No. Look. He *begs* me to pitch to him. You should come watch. That's a very happy kid out there. And I'm tellin' ya, he's a natural."

"Now, *that* word makes me *very* nervous."

"All I'm saying is, the kid was born with a gift, with tremendous hitting instinct."

"Instinct. I see."

"I know what you're thinking."

"Do you?"

"Instinct versus intelligence, all that. But hey, Jackie Robinson was a very intelligent man. And what better role model for a kid who wants to be a ballplayer, you know?"

"Did Darryl tell you that? That he wants to be a ballplayer?"

"Not in so many words. But all you gotta do is see him out there. He loves it."

"*I* loved playing baseball at his age, too. And I also loved playing nurse. And reading books."

"With all due respect, Miriam—"

She holds up her hand. "Keep your respect. The point is, it's up to Darryl what he wants to be, and I think you're trying to make that decision *for* him. So. Here's the deal. You let him play Martin Luther King. Give Jackie Robinson to James."

I shake my head, no.

I'm not sure why I'm being so stubborn. I guess I don't trust Darryl to decide on his own to be a ballplayer. He needs guidance. And anyway I don't like Miriam telling me what to do with him. He's *my* project.

"Sorry," I tell her.

"I see," she says. "Well. In that case, I'm afraid you can no longer work here."

"You're kidding."

"I assure you, I'm not."

"You're firing me?"

"That's correct."

"I'm a *volunteer*."

"No longer."

"Fine. I was quitting anyway. Did you know that?"

"No, I didn't."

"I *might* be willing to stay, under one condition: Darryl plays Jackie Robinson."

"Sorry."

"Then I'm afraid I can no longer work here."

"Your resignation is accepted."

* * *

On my way to the Greyhound Bus depot, I go up an extra block to Lambert Road so I can walk with my two suitcases and sad face past the school playground. The day is turning cool, the sun going in and out. A little drizzle, of course, would be perfect.

As usual the place is crawling with kids. I don't look for him. I just walk by very slowly, head lowered, suitcases almost skimming the sidewalk.

Sure enough, before I reach the end of the block I hear behind me, "Mister Butthead!"

I slowly set down my suitcases and slowly turn around.

"Where you going?" he says, standing there about ten yards aways, arms at his sides.

"I'm going home, Darryl. To Chicago. Where I'm from. Goodbye."

I want to break his little heart.

"Whaddaya got in there?" he says, pointing at the suitcases, sounding not at all heartbroken.

"Clothes," I tell him. "And my baseball glove," I add.

"You were gonna get *me* one."

"I know I was. But I can't now."

"Why not?"

"Because Miriam said I have to leave." I hold back from adding *Thanks to you*, and pick up my suitcases and walk slowly away.

"Hey!"

I keep walking.

"Mister Butthead!"

I suddenly realize I'll never see Darryl again.

I turn around and tell him to come here.

He walks up, a little cautiously, and stands before me. I get down and put my hands on his shoulders: "Darryl, listen to me, okay?"

He nods.

But I'm not sure what I want to tell him, what I want him to know. I ask him to give me a hug and he puts his strong little arms around my neck. "I'm gonna miss you," I tell him. *That's* what I want him to know.

"Will you pitch to me?"

"I wish I could, Darryl."

"Please?"

"I can't. I'm sorry. I really am."

"Please, Mister Butthead?"

"Darryl . . . "

"*Pleeease?*"

"Darryl, you're choking me."

* * *

As I sit there staring out the window on the bus trip home, it occurs to me that I'm turning out to be kind of a failure. Kind of a butthead, in fact.

Instructor, Composition Skills
CENTRAL Y COMMUNITY COLLEGE
CHICAGO 1976

So I go back to grad school and finish my degree and land a job at a two-year college down on Wacker and LaSalle, find a studio apartment, open a savings account, buy all new underwear, and get a girlfriend.

Her name is Patty Anderson. She's the secretary-receptionist in the English office. She seems extremely well-organized and efficient, a person who leaves nothing to chance. I like that. To hell with chance.

And she almost looks a little bit like Mary Tyler Moore, from a certain angle.

* * *

We eat lunch together in the school cafeteria. She tells me about her day so far and I tell her about mine. After we're finished eating she often tells me a joke, like dessert. It's never very funny but the food here isn't very good, so it seems right. And I always manage to laugh.

"That's very funny," I tell her. "I'll have to remember that one."

"Laughter is good for the digestion," she points out.

"Yes, I've read that somewhere."

"Would you like to hear another one?"

"We should probably be going."

* * *

At the door of her apartment building following our fifth date, she says, "We can start sleeping together now, if you'd like."

I tell her I would, very much.

In bed she informs me that she enjoys being kissed on the neck, especially just below the jaw line, and that she has very sensitive breasts. She says if I wish to excite her, those would be good areas to work on.

I go to work on those areas.

"I'm ready now," she says.

* * *

My students seem extremely lazy, sloppy and scatterbrained. I start requiring them to include a formal outline with their final draft. I declare war on digression. And I ask Lorenzo Ruiz to remove his hat. He looks at me like I'm crazy, but removes it.

I tell Patty that night: "So I said to him, 'Hey. Get rid . . . of the lid.'"

"And did he?"

"*Oh* yeah."

"Good for you, honey."

We call each other "honey."

* * *

Patty and I decide we're in love and that I should move into her apartment. And if that works out, we should get engaged in the spring and married in the summer. We set up a joint savings account. We buy a used car, a little blue and white Nash. And we have a child, sort of.

His name is Malcolm. He's actually a teddy bear Patty's had since she was little. She wants to have a real child exactly one year and nine months after we're married. Until then, this is our practice child.

She shows me how to burp him. I lay the dish towel over my shoulder and pat him gently but firmly on the back. And I swear I hear him give a tiny belch near my ear.

I learn to change his diapers, holding my breath.

* * *

Lorenzo Ruiz returns, hat in hand, after having missed his fourth class already this semester. I've given them three as the limit, no excuses acceptable. So I have to inform him that he's no longer in the class.

He says his father was shot. "Damn near killed him, man."

I tell him I'm sorry to hear that.

"So I'm okay, right?"

I tell him I'm sorry.

"This is my *father*, man."

I repeat that I'm very sorry.

If I make an exception for him, *everyone's* father will be shot, and I can't let that happen.

Lorenzo puts his face close to mine, says something in Spanish, and leaves the room.

Maybe he said, "Have a nice day."

* * *

As a little girl Patty had asthma, so there's a possibility our child will be asthmatic. So Malcolm has asthma. We make sure he sleeps on his back—in his open dresser drawer, under his little blue blanket—and now and then we have to hold him over a pot of boiling water, letting him breathe in the steam.

I haven't said anything, but I'm getting a little tired of Malcolm. Just a little bit.

One evening in the living room while I'm working on a stack of essays and Patty's reading *Parents* magazine and Malcolm's playing around on the floor, she suddenly says, "Oh my God," scoops him up and hands him to me. "He's got a penny caught in his throat!"

This is something that could happen to our Real Child, is the idea. But like I said, I'm getting tired of Malcolm. So I whack him a few times on the back and return him, telling her, "Honey, I'm sorry. I did all I could."

"What are you *saying*?

I can't go through with it. You should see her face. I tell her he's fine. "He swallowed it," I tell her.

She hugs him with huge relief. Then she looks at him and pokes his tummy: "You think you're a little piggy bank? Is that what you think? Hmmm?"

* * *

Lorenzo Ruiz comes up to me one cold evening on the street as I'm walking to the bus stop after my last class.

"Teacher! Hey!" He looks happy to see me.

"Lorenzo. Hi. How are you?"

"I'm good, man. How *you* doing?"

"Fine. How's your father?"

"My father?"

"The one that got shot."

"Oh, yeah. He's okay. The bullet, you know, it went right through."

"Glad to hear it. Well . . . "

"Ask you a question?"

"All right."

"You got something against Chicanos, man?"

"No, I don't."

"That's good. I thought maybe you did, you know?"

"Lorenzo, look . . . "

"See you around, man, okay?"

* * *

Two in the morning Patty shakes me awake and says, "Will you get him, honey? I'm so tired."

I don't know what she's talking about. Maybe she's still asleep.

But she's not. She wants me to get up and take Malcolm out of his bed—the open dresser drawer—and walk him around the apartment because he's crying hysterically.

I tell her he's probably hungry. Patty enjoys feeding him, with her sensitive breasts.

She says no, he isn't hungry, he's had a nightmare.

I've about had it with this bear.

I tell her, "Patty, listen to me. Malcolm doesn't have night-mares. He doesn't *dream*, you know?"

She says I'm wrong about that. "Babies begin dreaming early on."

"Babies, yes. But not teddy bears. They can't. They're made out of stuffing."

She gets angry. "I am well aware of the fact that Malcolm is a teddy bear, but I am also aware that we'll be having a *real* child someday—and *then* what?"

"Then I promise I'll get up when he's crying and walk him around."

She's glad to hear it, but shouldn't we begin getting used to the idea? "We can't just pretend Malcolm's our child when it's convenient. If there's one thing about a Real Child, it's never very *convenient*."

"Patty . . ."

"Never mind. Stay in bed. I'll get him."

"I got him, I got him, I got him," I tell her and get up and grab him out of his drawer and go pacing up and down the living room, holding him by one leg, swinging him a little, letting his head bang against the coffee table.

"Oh . . . my . . . God," she says from the bedroom doorway.

"Take it easy, take it easy," I tell her, and carry him properly.

"*Jiggle* him a little," she says. "He likes that."

* * *

I keep running into Lorenzo on the street. I'm beginning to think it's not by accident. I think he enjoys our little conversations. I think he knows he makes me nervous.

"How's the class going?" he asks me one evening.

"Oh, fine," I tell him.

He sighs. "Those were the days, man. I was happy, you know? Getting an education. Going somewhere. The future was looking *good*."

"Lorenzo, you were flunking. You hadn't even turned in a paper yet, not one."

"I was getting ready to—a *big* paper, you know? Hundred pages, man. About life on the street. What it's *really* like. It was gonna blow your mind."

"You could still write it."

"What for? I'm gettin' outa here."

"Oh?"

"I got a cousin down in Phoenix."

"Arizona?"

"That's right, man. He's givin' me a job."

I tell him that's wonderful. "I envy you. I really do. All
that sun. All that good heat."

"*Dry* heat," he adds.

"The best kind."

"You wanna come, man?"

"Hey, I'm tempted."

* * *

Malcolm begins growing older, faster and faster. He's in and
out of the terrible two's in a few days. Then he's "fwee years
ode." Then he's *this* many, Patty holding up four fingers
behind his paw. Then he's in kindergarten, where the other
boys pick on him because he's so small—tiny, in fact.

I tell Patty I think we're going to have to face the fact
that our son is a midget.

Lately when I say things like that she gives me this scru-
tinizing look, to see if I'm raising a possible Real Child issue
or making fun of her.

She usually decides I'm making fun of her.

* * *

My students' papers have shown a certain improvement and
I tell them about it. The papers are definitely, without a doubt,
more clearly organized than before. I also tell them, as nicely
as I can, that their papers have become more and more boring as well.

I mention it one evening to Lorenzo, who's still around.
I've lost a lot of my nervousness with him.

He says he's not surprised their papers are boring. "Buncha boring *people*, man. What do you expect?"

"I don't think that's it."

"Then maybe it's you, man. It's like paint-by-numbers with you, you know? My grandmother, she used to do that shit."

"Paint by numbers?"

"About one a day. She had 'em all over the walls. Clowns, and little girls with baskets, and birds on a branch, and some deers drinking from a creek—I *hated* those pictures, man. She'd show me the box, with the picture on it, you know? And then the picture *she* did, right? She'd say, 'See?' And I'd be thinking, *Why don't you just hang the box on the wall? Save you the trouble.* I'm freezing, man. Gimme a dollar, will you?"

"What for?"

"So I can go. I'm freezing."

* * *

Patty and I are in the middle of making love when she whispers hotly in my ear, "He's watching us."

She means Malcolm.

I roll off her. "Where is he? Where *is* he, Patty?"

She glances towards the closet, where the sliding door is open about an inch. I start to get up but she says, "Honey, don't. Come on. *Think* about it."

She's right. What am I, goofy? I'm pissed off at a teddy bear. I flop back down beside her. "You're right," I tell her.

She gives a sly little smile, lays her leg over me and whispers in my ear, "*You* were thirteen once. Didn't *you* like to spy?" She's pretty worked up. In fact, she's sort of writhing against me. I've never seen Patty writhe before.

I've always wanted a woman who writhes.

I whisper, "You little snake."

She likes that.

I go further: "You little slut."

That *really* sets her off and she gets on top, which she never does, and goes wild up there, glancing now and then towards the closet.

* * *

I tell all my classes I want them to write like mad for twenty minutes. I tell them I don't care what they write about, where they go with it, where it leads. Just write. "You never know what's down there," I tell them. "So just start putting words on the page and see what happens. See what comes up."

They want to know if this will be graded.

"Yes." Or else they won't put out.

They want to know how I'll determine the grade.

It's a fair question, but I don't want to answer it. Instead I tell them about my Aunt Mary and her paint-by-numbers kit, how I used to think to myself, *Why don't you just hang the box on the wall? Save yourself the time and trouble.*

They don't get it.

"Just start writing," I tell them.

* * *

Patty comes up to me as I walk in the door. She looks very upset. I hope it's not Malcolm. She takes my hand and leads me towards the bathroom. "I got home and found him like this," she says.

I'm hoping he's hanged himself.

He's lying face down over the toilet, apparently barfing his little guts out. There's an empty wine bottle on the floor.

"What're we going to do with him?" she says, leaning against me, all limp and weepy. I can smell the wine on her breath. "Honey," she says, "what're we gonna *do?*"

I tell her it's going to be all right. I hold her and tell her everything's going to be fine.

"Where did we go wrong?" she says.

I tell her I'm not sure.

* * *

I explain to Professor Reynolds that I won't be able to return for the spring semester. I tell him I have to go to Arizona.

"It's my little boy. He's asthmatic. The doctor says the dry climate can make a real difference."

He says he understands.

I have a feeling he knows I've been living all semester with his receptionist-secretary, that the little boy is really a teddy bear, and that I'm running out on them.

Afterwards, I stop at Patty's desk and she gives me a sheet of paper on which she's calculated exactly how much money I owe her for the Nash, which I can take, minus half the cost of items for the apartment we purchased together, plus compensation for the emotional damage of my leaving her. I would like to ask her about that last figure, which is a hundred and forty-eight dollars and thirty-seven cents. I'm not saying it's too high. I'm just curious, that's all.

We shake hands. I want to say something nice, something encouraging. "I never told you this, Patty, but I've always thought you look a little bit like Mary Tyler Moore, from a certain angle."

"Thank you," she says quietly.

* * *

Driving across Illinois, I tell the whole sad story of me and Patty and Malcolm.

"You shoulda let him choke on that penny, man," Lorenzo says. "You had the right idea there."

Field Worker

"You really hit it hard this morning, Teacher."

We're sipping beers under the moon, in reclining lawn chairs, poolside at an apartment down the road from ours, alone except for a fat guy doing laps with barely a splash.

Lorenzo means my head. I keep forgetting to duck it as I climb into the back of the canopied truck that takes us out to the fields. Not to make excuses, but it's dark at five in the morning and I'm still half-asleep. Anyway, about every other morning I smack my skull on an overhead beam. The other workers—all Mexicans—call me Bobo. Lorenzo says it means Idiot.

This morning they called me lots of other things too.

"What was everyone *yelling* at me for?"

"They were pissed off, man. Some of them."

"All I did was hit my head."

"That's right."

"I do it every morning."

"Not every morning," he corrects.

"Every *other* morning."

"Just about," he says.

"So?"

"So today was Monday, so it was hard to tell if you would or not. But now you did, so tomorrow you probably won't. Except, tomorrow you will. Tomorrow you're gonna hit your head. So remember."

"It's *ducking* my head I'm trying to remember."

"Just do it, man."

"Hit my head."

"Right."

"Wanna tell me why?"

"You have to know every fucking thing, man?"

We're quiet. I'm thinking.

"Lorenzo?"

"What."

"Are people laying bets on whether or not I hit my head?"

He takes a drink from his beer.

"Christ," I mutter. "How long's *this* been going on?"

"Since this morning. Couple guys lost their whole day's pay, thanks to you."

"*My* fault?"

"Well, what the hell, you can't remember to duck your head?"

"You bet your whole day's pay?"

"It was stupid, man. I shoulda waited."

"So we could set something up, you mean?"

"That's right. So hit it good, you know? Like this morning. Don't fake it."

"Forget it, Lorenzo. You tell them I know what's going on. Tell them from now on I will always duck my head."

"After tomorrow."

"*Starting* tomorrow."

He sits up. "Teacher, listen to me. I'm the only one who says you're gonna hit your head tomorrow. Everyone else— ten guys, man—they're all betting the other way. I can win a hundred dollars. And here's the best part: you get twenty- five of it. A whole day's pay for bumping your head. That's not so bad, you know?"

"Sorry."

"All right, *thirty*-five, but that's it, man."

"I'm not doing it."

He studies me. "Why are you being such a bobo?"

I give a large sigh. "Lorenzo, I don't know if you can understand this, but I happen to have something called scruples. It comes from having something called a con- science."

"I have something called an ass and you can kiss it, man. You think you're better than me? A better *person*, man? Fuck you, Teacher."

"I didn't say I was necessarily—"

"Fuck you, Bobo."

We're quiet.

The fat guy is doing the backstroke now, his big wet belly shining in the moonlight.

"Anyway, don't they know you know me? Won't they suspect something?"

"They don't know shit, man. Do I ever walk to the truck with you? Eat lunch with you? *Speak* to you?"

"No. You don't."

"Know why?"

"Let me guess. Because I'm a bobo."

"That's right, man. And don't ever forget it."

We're quiet again.

I stare at the moon, feeling sorry for myself, out there all day yanking away at some rubbery goddam tangled-up vine, bush after bush, row after row, no one to talk to but myself, known only as Bobo, as Idiot . . .

I ask Lorenzo what other names the men were calling me this morning.

"In English?"

"Please."

"Let's see . . . they said you were an asshole . . . a fornicator of goats . . . the son of a whore . . . the *daughter* of a whore . . . an eater of donkey shit . . . a stuck-up gringo bigot . . . "

"*Bigot?*"

"That's right."

I sit up. "Based on what?"

"Your attitude, man. With your scruples. Too good to talk to a buncha wetbacks."

"I don't speak *Spanish*, Lorenzo—remember?"

"That's very convenient, man."

"Jesus." I lie back and drink.

"There's that attitude. There it is, right there."

"Excuse me." It's the fat guy, standing near us in the shallow end, hands at his hips like a hardass. "Do you fellows live here?"

"What's it to you, man?"

I wave him away: "Do some more laps."

"Because if you *don't* live here—"

"Look at how *fat* you are," Lorenzo says. "You're like a fucking whale, you know that?"

The guy stands there a moment, slowly nodding his head, like he knows what to do about us, then gets out and grabs his towel and marches off.

Lorenzo yells insulting things about the size of his butt.

"He's gonna call security," I point out.

"Let's go."

I start putting the empties in the carton.

"Leave that shit for him."

I leave it.

"Take the *box*, man. There's some beers left."

"Right." I take the carton.

He stands there shaking his head at me.

"Don't," I tell him.

"Don't what, man."

"Call me a bobo."

He laughs.

"I mean it, Lorenzo. I don't like it. I'm not an idiot. I have a goddam *Masters* degree, you know?"

"So what should I call you? Master?"

"I'm serious."

"I know, man. That's your whole problem."

We head down the moonlit gravel road, palm trees on either side.

"Give me one of those," he says.

I hand him a beer from the carton. He pops it open and takes a long drink, belches and sighs. "You know what I should *really* call you, man?"

"No more names. Please."

"You'll like this one." He puts his arm around my shoulder. "Amigo. That's what I should call you. You know what *that* word means, don't you?"

"Friend."

"That's right, man. And don't ever forget it."

It's a little embarrassing with his arm around my shoulder like that, but I feel glad we're amigos—happy, in fact. "Guess we told *that* fatass, didn't we?"

"Hey, I bet that guy can really stink up a bathroom, man. You know?"

We laugh like amigos.

Then he gets serious. "Hey, listen. About tomorrow. Don't forget. Okay?"

"What."

"You forgot already. Bump your *head*, man."

I slip out from under his arm.

"What's the matter?" he says.

I don't answer.

"Listen, man, don't let me down. It's not just the money, you know? It would hurt my *feelings*. I would feel like . . . what's the word?"

"Betrayed."

"I would feel like betrayed. You know what I mean by betrayed?"

"I just gave you the word."

"I know. My English, it is not so good," he says, his accent suddenly thicker. "Maybe if I had more school. But it was not to be."

"Don't start that."

He goes on, "You know, amigo, that day when you told me I could no longer be in your class anymore, it was like you were telling me I could no longer be in your *world* anymore, that I must always remain a poor ignorant Chicano."

"My attendance policy was very clear."

He sighs. "So now I must work in the fields, where I belong."

"Hey, *I'm* in the fields and I was the *teacher*."

"Yeah, but you're a fucking bobo, man."

"Right. I keep forgetting."

We walk on.

"Listen, I didn't mean that, man. Still amigos, right? Okay?"

* * *

When I duck my head the next morning, there are sounds all around of satisfaction and gratitude. And as I sit on the bench an old man to my right says quietly, "Buenos días, Señor Bobo."

"Buenos días," I say to him, a little lump in my throat.

Lorenzo lets go a yell, steps up and grabs me by the front of my T-shirt, pulls me to my feet, swings me around and throws me out the back.

The truck is going slow along a sandy road, so all I do is skin my elbows and drive a lot of grit up under my fingernails. I get to my feet and stand there in the dark watching the tail lights growing smaller.

Maybe he meant that stuff about being amigos. This seems pretty extreme just for money.

I begin walking after the truck.

Tutor

Aug 20, 1978

Dear Lorenzo,

*I'm leaving. I can't take this job
another day. It's just too goddam
hot out there.*

*I sincerely hope you have a very
pleasant life.*

Your amigo,
Teacher

I take 17 up to Flagstaff, then 40 over to Albuquerque, then 25 up to Denver. There's some beautiful scenery along the way and I try to pay attention and appreciate it. But I'm feeling very ghostly. I feel like I could slip into being dead with hardly a ripple.

I take 80 east, which goes to Chicago, but at North Platte, Nebraska, I get on 83 north. I don't know where I want to go but I don't want to go back to Chicago.

I hit a town called Valentine, just before the South Dakota border. It's after dark as I park my little Nash between
two pickup trucks and walk into a bar called Diamond Jack's.
Country Western music is playing and a woman on a little
stage is taking off her clothes. I find a stool and order a beer
and watch her. She isn't very attractive but she seems to be
enjoying herself.

At a table in front of the stage a bunch of guys in cowboy hats are whistling and hooting and laughing and tilting
their chairs back and slugging one another in the arm. They
seem to be imitating cowboys in a beer commercial. You
could argue it's the other way around, but that's not my
impression.

When the girl gets down to her g-string and pasties—
apparently as far as the law here allows—she doesn't seem
to know what else to do. So she starts doing jumping-jacks.
I'm serious. She has great big tits and they're flopping and
wheeling like mad and the cowboys are hooting and hollering
like cowboys and I finish my beer and get back on the road.

I continue north, into South Dakota, onto the Rosebud
Indian Reservation, into a little town called St. Francis, and
knock on a trailer with lights in the windows, to ask directions to the nearest motel, hoping a wise old medicine man
invites me in and we smoke a peace pipe and he teaches me
the ways of the Red Man and gives me an Indian name,
something like *Many Roads* or *Many Jobs*.

An old skinny baldheaded very pale-faced paleface in
thick glasses, a narrow black tie and suspenders opens the
door. He *is* smoking a pipe, and he's very friendly.

"Hello. Come in," he says. "Welcome to the Rosebud. Would you like something to drink? I have some lemonade. Why don't you ask your wife to join us."

"Actually, I don't have one," I say, apologetically.

"I see. Well, now I'm confused. I was told you were bringing a wife."

"I think you're mistaking me for someone else, sir." I tell him my name and how haphazard my being here is.

"I thought you were the new history teacher. I was told he was coming out early, being something of an Indian enthusiast. You're still welcome to some lemonade, if you'd like."

"Thank you."

"'A Persian's heaven is easily made. 'Tis but black eyes and lemonade.'"

"Pardon?"

"From Thomas Moore, early 19th century. Sit at the table. My name is George Burns, by the way—like the comedian, only I smoke a pipe instead of a cigar and I'm not very funny, at least not intentionally. Here you are."

"Thank you."

He stands by my chair. "In fact, I'm told that the students refer to me as Mister Death. I assume it's because I resemble a cadavar, dress like a mortician and teach mathematics, which is dry like old bones."

"High school?"

"I'm afraid so."

"Do you know if they need any English teachers?"

"Not to my knowledge. But they may be needing people for the new tutoring center. You should speak to a man named Bob Sage. So. You're an English teacher. Do you think someone else wrote Shakespeare's plays?"

"No."

"I quite agree. You can sleep here tonight, if you like. I'm not a homosexual."

*   *   *

It's past noon when I wake up on George Burns's lumpy corduroy couch. He's in the kitchen, a few feet away, talking to a big brown broadfaced Indian in a T-shirt and John Deere cap, who comes right over when he sees me sit up, shakes my hand, says his name is Ben Walking Eagle, and asks if I like baseball.

"Yes," I tell him. "I do."

He asks if I need a glove.

"Well, no. I've got one in the car, in the trunk."

He tells me to hurry up and get dressed.

He explains on the way, driving George and me in his pickup truck along a dusty gravel road that rolls through miles of nothing but grassland. Game time is in half an hour. Three of their players—including their best hitter, Ben's cousin Charlie Bad Hand—were in a car accident last night driving back from Cut Meat. No one was killed but they're all in the hospital, leaving the team with eight guys, and he wasn't able to recruit anyone because no one wants to risk it.

"Risk what?"

"Screwing up. This is a big game. We're playing the Negroes."

I'm not sure I heard him correctly. "The who?"

"The Negroes. They're from Mission. They're not really Negroes. That's just their team name, you know?"

George says, "As, for example, Redskins, Chiefs, Indians, Braves . . ."

"We're the Jews," Ben says.

Seems fair enough.

* * *

The field is laid out in the middle of nowhere, with cars parked every which way, and Indians everywhere—on the hoods and roofs of the cars, packed into a pair of rickety bleachers, and some on actual horses. Little kids are racing around, dogs chasing them, and there's a couple of tables with women selling quilts and cookies.

The field isn't bad. It has a freshly-dragged dirt infield with a well-built pitcher's mound. The outfield grass needs cutting but hopefully I'll be in the infield, where I belong. They've got cement block dugouts, a good backstop, and up behind it a wooden shaky-looking announcer's booth where a fat guy in a straw cowboy hat with a big white feather is chatting away over a loudspeaker.

Ben turns off the engine and says, "Right field or second base—which you want?"

"Second base, definitely. I've always—"

He gets out and hurries off towards the announcer's booth.

George gets out, carefully climbs up on the hood and lights his pipe. I get out and stand there with my glove.

"Last-minute addition for the Jews," the announcer says. "A *wasichu*!"

There's some polite applause.

I look at George.

He removes his pipe. "Means white man."

Ben yells something at me, cupping his mouth, and I open my arms and shake my head, meaning I didn't hear, and he yells something up to the announcer, who speaks again:

"He doesn't seem to have a name. So: batting ninth, playing second base for the Saint Francis Jews: No-Name.

There's some laughter.

I look at George.

He shrugs.

"Okay, folks," the announcer continues, "just about ready to get started. Couple messages. Ellen One Feather, if you're here . . . "

I've gone from Idiot to No-Name. That seems the right direction. And it's certainly a beautiful day for a ballgame.

Ben waves me over and I follow him to the third base dugout to meet my fellow Jews.

* * *

The P.A. guy never shuts up, as if he's covering the game over radio. He's pretty good though:

"Here's the wind-up and the first pitch of the game—a *strike*, says umpire Bill Many Horses, right on the outside corner. Nice pitch, Ben. Sally Iron Shell just gave us some good news from the hospital: all three are listed in good condition. Happy to hear that. If you seen what their car looked like—here's an easy fly ball out to left field, Eddie Red Water under it . . . for the out."

As we throw the ball around the infield, I have to work hard at keeping a stupid grin off my face. I mean, here I am, playing baseball on an Indian reservation in South Dakota. I feel like I'm leading a pretty damn colorful life.

The game turns out to be a pitcher's duel. I make a couple of handy fielding plays, receiving a nice response from the crowd. At the plate though, I whiff my first time up and ground out in my next appearance. But in the bottom of the eighth, with still no score, I push a perfect little bunt up the first base line and easily beat it out.

Lots of cheering, and the announcer says, "Well done, No-Name! Well done!"

I'm quickly becoming a local favorite.

The batter after me hits a weak grounder to the shortstop, who throws to second base, and I slide in hard to break up the double play.

The second baseman is hurt. He's on his back, holding his knee, rocking from side to side with his eyes closed. Other Negro players are gathered around him, speaking to him in Indian. He looks up at me and says something. I ask the guy beside me to translate.

"Said you better go on back home, *wasichu*."

"Tell him I'm very sorry. Tell him I—"

"He speaks English."

"Right. Listen," I say to the guy, bending over him, "I am very sorry. Okay? Not personal. Part of game. Okay?"

He shakes his head, apparently meaning it's not okay.

And as I trot back to the dugout all the fans are booing me. They're mostly Jew fans and the guy's a Negro, but I guess more importantly I'm a white man and he's an Indian.

The announcer is curiously quiet.

None of my teammates congratulate me for breaking up the double play and in fact don't even look at me.

The runner makes it to third on a base hit, then scores on a fly ball to center field—which would have been the third out if I hadn't broken up the double play, but that doesn't seem to occur to anyone.

We go out for the ninth, ahead 1-0. Ben strikes out the first batter, gets the next one to fly to right, and I have the honor of gloving an easy pop-up for the final out of the game. I figure on lots of shouting and jumping around and I'm all set to—but I'm glad I wait because the other Jews just trot over to Ben and shake his hand on a job well done, then drift off the field in different directions.

I'm standing on the mound still holding the ball. Then I suddenly realize: Here I am, a white man, a *wasichu*, alone among many braves, on their land, having *injured* one of them, standing here like Custer . . .

"Hey, Ben?" I catch up with him.

*   *   *

Riding back between Ben and George, I ask the name of the guy I hurt.

"Randy Kills Plenty," says Ben.

"That's his name?" I look at George. "That's really his name?"

He nods.

I turn to Ben. "These names. I'm curious. How's that work? I mean, do people *earn* them?"

"You bet."

"Okay, but for example, this Kills Plenty guy . . . I'm just wondering . . ."

George explains that the names are generally handed down and refer to some incident or achievement involving a relative in the past.

"I see. So in other words the name isn't necessarily a good description of the person owning it *now*. Is that what you're saying?"

"Well," he says, "I have a very shy, polite boy in my algebra class whose name is Robert Respects Nothing."

I laugh. "That's funny."

"Do you think so?"

"No. Actually, it's kind of sad. Poor kid. But I get your point. These names aren't very accurate."

"Sometimes they are," Ben says.

I make it simple: "Kills Plenty. Accurate name or not?"

George says, "I'm sure he's never actually killed any-one."

"Not *plenty*, anyway," Ben adds.

* * *

Tomorrow is Monday and I want to go see this guy Bob Sage about a job at the tutoring center, so I stay again with George, who feeds me a cheese sandwich and tomato soup and lemonade. Afterwards I flop on his couch with one of his *Smithsonian* magazines and he goes to the room he calls his office to write some letters. Meanwhile, there's a pow-wow going on at the school gym. I think about going over there—how often do you get to see an authentic Indian pow-wow?—but I'm a little afraid of running into Randy Kills Plenty, so I stay on the couch. The gym's a good distance down the road but you can clearly hear the drumming and high wild eerie singing.

That night I dream I go to my high school prom with this girl I used to be in love with, Lucille Hanratty. She looks so beautiful with her bare shoulders and corsage, her hair piled up high and sprinkled with tiny stars. The theme this year is "Indian Days," featuring music performed by actual members of the Sioux tribe. I want to slow-dance to something romantic but we have to hop around like Indians while they drum and shout, "Hey-ah, hey-ah! Wey-ah, wey-ah!" But Lucille *enjoys* dancing like that, her makeup running, her hair toppling over. Then Randy Kills Plenty is standing in front of me with his arms folded. I immediately back away, all the way off the dance floor, then stand there watching as he turns to Lucille, who steps into his arms, and they begin slow-dancing while the Indians sing "Blue Moon."

* * *

I get a job in the tutoring center, helping kids with their writing assignments. I like it: no lesson plans or grades and the kids aren't obnoxious at all. I don't generally like kids, especially teenagers, but these are different. There's this deep reserve to them—some won't even make eye contact. It's like they give me a certain amount of themselves but that's all. The rest is Indian and I don't have access to that. Which is fine.

The other tutor's for math—a woman, Mary Big Bear, who isn't anything like her name. She's very slender and beautiful, like the Indian maiden on the label for Land o' Lakes butter. I try to get friendly with her but she doesn't like me. She doesn't think I care enough about the kids. So for a while I pretend that I do, telling her it breaks my heart to see what these children are up against. But I can tell she knows I'm full of shit and I give it up. She already has a boyfriend anyway, Albert Singer, a go-getter on the tribal council, pushing hard to get a John Deere factory out here. He's very tall and noble-looking, and I have to admit they make a handsome couple.

I live with George, in the room he was using as an office. I bought a mattress and pillow from the school and a beautiful quilted blanket from Delores Many Horses. Under the pillow I keep a long sharp hunting knife, in case of Randy Kills Plenty.

I got the knife off Mark in the next trailer—the history teacher George mistook me for. The guy's got quite an assorment of blades, along with two rifles, a bow and arrow, and a crossbow. He wears a buckskin jacket with fringe and goes hunting a lot with Ed Two Hats. Last week they brought back a deer, dead of course, and I sat on the steps with Mark's wife Cindy and watched them cut it up.

"I hate this place," she goes.

"My father's a butcher."

"I really and truly do."

She chain smokes and watches a lot of television and badgers Mark to take her to Rapid City on weekends.

My weekend spot is Diamond Jack's, in Valentine. I get reasonably drunk and usually manage to buy the dancer a drink and try talking her into going to bed with me. The only one who said yes to bed also said it would cost me twenty-five dollars. No way was I going to pay for it. And yet I did, and had a great time. Her name is Amy. She's there every two weeks.

Now and then Randy Kills Plenty appears in my dreams, always standing there with his arms folded while I back away. Otherwise, I've never seen him. He lives in Mission.

So all in all, this isn't too bad a life I have going here. I even have a savings account.

* * *

Then one afternoon I get very depressed.

It's Sunday in mid-November. I'm in my room, sitting at the desk with a piece of fry bread and one of George's *Smithsonian* magazines. I happen to look out the window. Shreds of dry-looking snow are darting around and this guy

Joe Hollow Horn Bear is walking down the road, hatless, hands jammed in his jacket pockets, hunching against the wind. And that's all. But for some reason I suddenly feel so miserable I want to lie right down and die.

I lie down. I don't die though, and the next morning it's still with me, like the flu. It doesn't seem to be about anything: I just feel very sorrowful. My heart actually feels heavy, literally. With a heavy heart I go to work, and when I get home I drag my heart back to bed.

This goes on all week.

On Friday night I drive to Diamond Jack's but I can't get drunk. Amy is there and after she's through dancing we go to her room, but I can't get it up.

"What's the problem?"

"I don't know. Got the blues."

She tells me I still have to pay.

I try talking to George about all this. He quotes from *Hamlet*: "'How weary, stale, flat and unprofitable seem to me all the uses of this world.'"

I tell him that's pretty much the feeling.

He informs me that the first production of *Hamlet*, at the Globe Theater, featured Shakespeare in the role of the Ghost.

I tell him I didn't know that, and go to bed.

Sunday night Mark walks up to my room with his heavy boots, knocks once, and tells me through the door that he's arranged for me to do an *inipi* the following evening and that we'll be leaving here at seven, and stomps off.

An *inipi* is a sweat lodge ceremony. It's supposed to be good for the soul. George must have told him about my condition.

So the next evening I'm in Mark's pickup truck, my hand braced against the glove box as we bounce along a dark hilly road.

"Now, don't be alarmed by the incredible intensity of the steam," he warns.

I don't care for his condescending tone and assure him I don't alarm easily.

"And don't take that attitude," he says. "This isn't a test of your manhood. An *inipi* is designed to purify and realign your spirit. Henry Crow is a genuine authentic shaman, and let me tell you, it's an extremely rare privilege for a *wasichu* to be allowed to sweat with him. I had to do a lot of talking to get you in."

I thank him.

It's a clear night with a big bright moon.

He goes on about Henry Crow, who's very old and blind and has tremendous *wochangi*. "Do you know what that is? *Wochangi*? Do you know what that word means?"

"Not exactly, no."

"*Wochangi* means spiritual power. With a shaman of Henry's advanced level it's like an energy field. So don't ever touch him. It could knock you unconscious. In fact, with a person at *your* level, it could kill you."

"Please don't squeeze the shaman—is that what you're saying?"

He stops the truck.

"I don't think you're ready for this," he says. "I'm going to take you back."

"Hey, a little joke. Take it easy. Jesus."

"Maybe you just need to get laid."

"I tried that."

"Because I'll tell you the truth: I have a hard time imagining you with any kind of crisis of the spirit, you know? Not to be insulting, but do you have any spiritual dimension at all? I'm serious."

"I used to be an altar boy," I tell him.

"An altar boy."

"'Course, that was long ago," I add.

He sighs and drives on.

I wasn't trying to be funny.

*   *   *

The sweat lodge is a dome about ten feet in diameter built out of willow branches, covered with canvas tarps and blankets, sitting on a snow-covered hill overlooking the town. Frank One Star is tending some loaf-sized rocks in a fire pit outside the lodge, moving them around with deer antlers, the rocks glowing pink. He tells us to get undressed and go on in.

We hang our clothes on the branch of a small tree, the moon easily bright enough to see by. Standing there in the snow, in my underpants, I promise myself I will someday lead a more normal life.

Mark crawls into the dome through an open flap and I follow him in. It's very dark.

"Over here, No-Name." Ben's voice.

I'm glad. I crawl over to him. The floor is covered with sage and smells wonderful. Ben pats the ground beside him and I sit there, feeling safe.

But then I have a thought. "Ben," I whisper, leaning close. "Is Randy Kills Plenty in here?"

He laughs.

"*Is* he?"

"No."

Frank One Star begins bringing in the hot rocks, carrying them on the deer antlers and setting them in a pit in the center of the room. They warm the place up nicely.

Then he closes the flap and there's total darkness. I don't like that. I feel lost in space, floating through the cosmos in my underpants.

Henry Crow begins singing. He has a voice like you'd expect from his name, but I'll tell you what, I've never heard anyone sing with so much *wochangi*. I don't know what he's singing, what the words mean, but he seems to be speaking directly to the Great Whatever, asking Him to kindly help us out of all this goddam darkness down here.

Afterwards he says, in English: "I'm told there's a new one here. No-Name? Is that what you're called?"

"That's—yes, right," I tell him across the dark.

"Good name. Good way to start. Maybe a good way to finish, too. I'm going to smoke on that. And the other *wasichu*, the one who comes a lot—he's here?"

"Yes, Tunkashila," Mark answers. "I am here."

"Don't call me that. I'm not your grandfather. That's from the movies."

I smile in the dark.

"Here's what we're gonna do, No-Name. We're gonna pass the pipe around now. When it comes to you, say a short prayer before you smoke. Just a little prayer. Something. Pray in your own way, we'll pray in ours. It's the same God. You know that."

The pipe goes around, each man saying a short something in Lakota. When it comes to Mark he says, *"Hau Mitakuye Oyasin."* I've heard the phrase before. It means, "To all my relations," which according to the Sioux means, "To all things."

It's a good prayer and when the pipe comes to me I say, "To all my relations," in English to show I'm not a wanna-be like Mark, and take a pull. I'm surprised. It tastes like a menthol cigarette. I hand the pipe to Ben and he speaks longer than the rest of us, in Lakota. I hear the name Stanley in there, so he's praying for his uncle Stanley Dancer, who blew his brains out last month.

When the pipe returns to Henry Crow, he starts singing again. I'm wishing we could just sit here listening to him and to hell with the rest of the ceremony. But I know what's going to happen next. He's going to begin ladling water from the bucket beside him and pouring it over the glowing rocks.

Don't be alarmed by the incredible intensity of the steam.
The song ends.

I want to leave. I feel all better now, completely over my silly depression.

I hear the scrape of the ladle in the bucket. I brace myself. Then I hear the hiss of the water hitting the rocks and the next moment I inhale a flame that goes down my throat and into my lungs and I grab Ben's arm.

"Go down," he tells me. "Breathe down there."

I put my face to the floor. He's right. There's air down here. Then another hiss, bigger than the first, and the flames find me down there and when I try to breathe I can't get any air. I try all around—no air, only fire—and I panic. I start crawling like mad over laps and legs towards the entrance. I don't give a shit. I have to breathe.

"*Wasichu* coming through," Ben announces.

Frank One Star opens the flap and I crawl out into the clear cold breatheable moonlit night.

"All right?" he asks.

"Yes," I answer, standing up. "I'm sorry," I tell him.

He closes the flap.

Henry Crow begins singing again.

I stand very still in the snow, in my underpants, listening.

* * *

"Mister No-Name!"

This girl Cheryl Little Elk comes up to me after school one afternoon while I'm walking back to the trailer, hunching against the January wind. She's with her friend Linda Kills In Water.

This is very unusual, a kid coming up to me. But she wants to show me the "A" on this paper she wrote. I helped her with some of the grammar and punctuation but that's about it.

"See?" she says, paying me the high compliment of assuming I'll be happy for her.

I tell her, "That's great, Cheryl. I'm really happy for you."

Walking off with her friend she says again, over her shoulder, "See?"

See what?

*   *   *

I'm helping Gary White Hat with an essay for his English class, trying to show him how to put together some kind of an outline. It's after three and we're the only ones in the room. Whatever I say to him he nods like he understands, but I only have to look in his eyes to see there isn't any point in continuing. He's definitely high on something, and the way he keeps sniffing and wiping his nose with his Nike wristband I think of cocaine, although that seems unlikely out here. Then I realize what that smell is: airplane glue. It's on his wrist band. *That's* what the sniffing is about.

I tell him we'll go on with this tomorrow. He starts to get up, but I ask him, "How's basketball?" He's a starting guard.

"Okay," he says.

"Who you playing tomorrow?"

"Not sure," he says, and gives his wristband a sniff.

"Gary . . ."

He waits.

"You seem a little . . . out of it today."

He shrugs.

"Hard to concentrate?"

He shrugs.

"Y'know, Gary . . . "

"Hey. I gotta go now." He gets up.

I tell him to sit down. "We need to talk."

He tells me I need to mind my own *wasichu* business, and walks out.

I sit there for a while. Then I write up a report to the principal Bob Sage and leave it in his box and go home.

The next day Bob leaves a note in my box, thanking me for my report, saying he'll write up a report. I don't know who he gives *his* to, but I have a feeling they'll write up a report . . .

* * *

Billy Lame Horse's father, Tom, comes to the trailer one Friday night in early spring, drunk as hell, saying he wants to talk to me and George about Billy, how he's doing in school:

"I wanna know. Good or bad. You tell me. I'll sit here. Go ahead. Got a beer?"

"No," I tell him.

"How's he doing? I'm listening. You go first," he says, pointing at George.

George tells him about Billy's classwork, that it's not bad, although he could do far better if he applied himself.

"What for? What's he gonna get? A big star on his head?"

"Well . . ."

"Hey. He ain't gonna leave the reservation. He's a good kid. He ain't going nowhere. So what's the difference? Hey. Listen. I was in Vietnam. You got a beer for me?"

I tell him I'm sorry, no.

"Gimme a damn beer. I'm a vet."

"We don't have any, Tom." It's the truth.

"I killed fourteen them sonofabitches, you know? Hey. Know what I used? No gun." He makes the motion of shooting a bow and arrow, with the sound: "Ffft." He looks at me. "You don't believe it?"

"I believe," I tell him.

"You think I'm a drunken Indian? You think I'm full a shit? Tell you something, both a you *wasichus*: *you're* full a shit. That's what *I* think. You know? I'm going to sleep. Tired a you people."

He stretches out on the couch and goes to sleep.

Late the next morning, Saturday, he sits up looking miserable. He apologizes for anything he said last night. "Talk kinda crazy when I'm drunk."

"Me, too," I say. I tell him not to worry about it.

"Tell you about Vietnam? The bow and arrow?"

"Yeah, but hey, like I said—"

"And the knife?"

"No, just the bow and arrow."

"I had a knife too. You know?" He grabs his hair and makes a scalping motion and a ripping sound. "I didn't tell you about that?" He's on his feet now. "Gimme two dollars. I gotta eat. Buy some soup."

George says he'll make some soup for him here, if he'd like, or he can take along some cans. "We've got vegetable. We've got—."

"I don't want your damn soup. I'm no charity case, man." He turns to me. "Gimme two dollars."

I give him three, and he leaves.

"He'll only use it to buy more alcohol," George says.

I watch Tom walking away. Watch him cross the gray road. Watch him stand there waiting for a car. Watch him standing there . . .

"So why shouldn't he?" I say to George. "What else is there for him, you know? What else is there for *anybody*? Do you know? Can you tell me? You know so goddam much. What *about* it?"

George works on his pipe, letting me rant on.

* * *

That night I go out and get pretty drunk myself.

Amy isn't in this week at Diamond Jack's—it's that big-titted girl doing jumping-jacks—so after a few beers I drive to Kilgore, to the Indian bar, what the hell.

Ben is there. "Hey! No-Name! Over here!" he tells me, like in the sweat lodge.

I step over someone asleep on the floor—it's Tom Lame Horse—and sit with Ben and his cousin Charlie Bad Hand, drinking Buddy Wisers, as they call them here. Charlie has his head wrapped in a hospital bandage. Every time I see the guy he's been in another car accident and has his leg in a cast or his neck in a brace or his arm in a sling—*something*. I ask about his head, what happened. He just grins and looks at Ben.

"Car," Ben says.

"He shouldn't be allowed to drive. No offense, Charlie."

He nods.

"He don't drive," Ben says. "That's the funny thing, you know? He always gets in the wrong car. Whatever car he's in, it's gonna crash. People stopped givin' him rides, you know? He's bad medicine. Poor Charlie, huh? Gotta walk everywhere."

Charlie sadly shakes his head.

"So how'd *this* happen?"

"Got swiped by a car. Knocked him flying. Show him your ribs."

Charlie lifts his dirty sweatshirt and shows me the bandages.

I buy him a beer.

I start drinking some shots with mine and get very drunk. I tell Ben and Charlie I understand why the Indian drinks the way he does. I tell them I understand the hopelessness, the feeling that there's no tomorrow so why not just get drunk, why not just drink yourself into an early grave and be goddam done with it.

Ben says, "Hey, listen, we're going to Tim White Tail's. You wanna come?"

"Sure. Why not? What's the difference?"

"Okay, but you're gonna have to quit talkin' like this.
You're kind of a *downer*, you know?"

* * *

The rest of the night is a little spotty.

I remember a lot of people in one room, all Indians, all
drinking beer. And I remember at some point Tim White
Tail, Ben, Charlie, and Frank One Star begin doing songs,
sitting on the floor around a big powwow drum, pounding
away, hollering their heads off.

I want to dance, so I do. I dance all around the drum-
mers, doing a little toe-heel, toe-heel, head up, head down.
Then someone is standing in my way, with his arms folded.
It's Randy Kills Plenty.

I stop dancing. The song ends. Everyone is quiet.

In the dream I'm always a coward. In the dream I always back away. But I'm not a coward and will not back
away. "I'm not afraid," I say to him. "If you wish to fight, I
am ready." And I strike my heart with my fist. "For it is a
good day to die."

This gets a loud response from everyone—mostly cheering, it seems.

Randy steps up and puts his hand on my shoulder. He
shakes his head. "I can't fight you," he says.

"Why not?"

"*Because*, man. You're too fucking silly."

Outside, it's dark and raining hard as I get into my Nash.
I head back towards Valentine, towards white people, driv-

ing fast. Suddenly someone appears in the headlights, standing there grinning: Charlie Bad Hand. *But he's back at the party, drumming and singing.* I whip the wheel and stomp on the brakes.

I remember skidding, the tree coming fast, remember at the last moment thinking this is a *terrible* day to die.

Umpire

The guy in the other bed fell asleep during *Charlie's Angels*, so when this nice old volunteer nurse named Abby passed the door I called her in and asked if she would look for a ballgame.

She found Tommy Lasorda yelling at the home plate umpire.

"*Well* now," she said, "*he* doesn't look very pleased."

"Thanks, Abby," I told her, wanting to watch this.

"So how ya feelin' today, hon?"

"Fine. Thanks."

"If you need anything else, you just—"

"I will. Thank you."

Lasorda had his cap turned sideways so he could get right up in the guy's face, the ump just letting him vent, looking a little bored, in fact. But Lasorda must have said something special because all of a sudden, just like that, the ump threw him out. And after a few more words Lasorda marched off, tossing remarks over his shoulder, the ump ignoring him now, putting his mask back on, pointing at the pitcher to go ahead and throw. And the game resumed.

I never really thought about umpires before, but that was quite cool how he handled that. I especially admired the way he pointed at the pitcher, like saying, *Yes, I'm the boss. Now let's move on.*

The rest of the game I kept my eye on him. I enjoyed his strike-three call, like starting up a chain saw, and tried it out—a mistake, with my ribs.

But they were getting better. So was the neck and the knee. And after the game I lay there thinking.

Next day I made some phone calls.

*   *   *

"You're the boss," I whisper.

I'm in the parking lot at the trunk of my Nash, getting ready for tonight's game, my very first behind the plate: cup, shin guards, chest protector, ball bag, brush, clicker, breath mints.

"You . . . are . . . the *boss.*"

I grab my mask, slam the trunk, and stride on out to the field.

*   *   *

In the pre-game ground-rules meeting at home plate, I introduce myself to the opposing coaches and we shake hands. They both know the base umpire—Butter, short for Butterball—and all three stand around joking about his beer gut. I give them a minute before interrupting:

"Gentlemen, if we can get started here?"

They trade looks.

Let them. I'm the boss.

*   *   *

After thoroughly brushing off the plate, I step behind the catcher, shout "*Play ball*," and here we go, here it comes: my first pitch.

Outside corner at the knees.

"*Striiike*," and I punch air.

The batter gives me a look but no lip.

I remember to click "strike" on my indicator.

Next one's a tad low and I grunt, "*Ball.*"

The catcher leaves his glove there, trying to show me up.

"Let's go," I tell him, and he tosses the ball back.

Then a foul out of play and I grab a new ball from the bag at my hip and fire it out to the mound.

"*One ball, two strikes!*" I announce, holding up the appropriate fingers.

Then an off-speed pitch and the batter freezes, the ball cuts the inside corner of the plate knee-high and I start up a chain saw, hollering, "*Haaa!*"

Meaning, *Strike three, go sit down, I'm the boss.*

*   *   *

Two innings go by with barely a peep out of anyone. They can see how locked-in I am, how absolutely certain: that's a strike, that's a ball. Not opinions, facts.

Then in the third inning a close play at the plate, all dust and limbs, but the runner's in under the tag and I fling out my arms crying "*Saaaafe!*"

The catcher throws a tantrum, jumping up and down in front of me: "*No! No! No! No!*"

I hold up my hand and tell the fellow, "Enough. Let's go. Play ball." And the game resumes.

I'm pretty sure I know what Butter over there is thinking by now:

This guy is good.

* * *

Then in the sixth inning I call a strike on the outside corner and the batter turns to me with a look, not of anger, but of genuine amazement: "Are you *serious?*" he says.

I tell him I'm quite serious. But the look on his face concerns me a little, just a tiny little bit.

The next pitch is exactly as close but on the *inside* corner and for a moment I hesitate.

"*Ball,*" I decide.

"*What?*" cries the pitcher, with the same genuine amazement as the batter on the previous pitch.

And am I imagining this or is the batter *smirking* to himself, thinking he influenced my call? If that's the case, I'd like to assure him he is very much mistaken. And although the next pitch is low I decide it may have caught the knees.

"*Striiike!*"

He drops his arms and shakes his head at the darkness above the lights, his teammates in the third base dugout speaking for him.

"At his *ankles*, blue!"

"That sucks!"

"Get in the game!"

I don't look. The call did not suck. The pitch was at his knees. Or thereabouts. And anyway, what about all the *good* calls I've made?

The next pitch is very high and outside.

"*Ball.*"

"Good eye, ump!" from a sarcastic fan.

I don't hear it.

Yes, I do.

The next one is inside and I call it a ball and nobody squawks and I feel in control again after a little bumpy stretch there. "*Full count*," I announce, holding up three-and-two fingers.

All right, here we go, you're the boss, here it comes . . .

It's high.

A little.

I think.

Or is it.

I don't know.

Call *something*.

"*Striiike!*"

The batter slams his bat on the plate. "You are fucking *pitiful*," he tells me, and stalks back to the dugout.

I don't have to take that. It's one thing to say the *call* is pitiful, but to say *I* am pitiful, and not just pitiful but *fucking* pitiful . . .

I should eject him, I know. But I stand there, hands on my hips, feeling pitiful.

* * *

After the inning Butter comes strolling over. "Don't let these guys get to you. Just start tossing 'em."

I give a laugh and tell him this is nothing. I tell him he should try umping winter ball in Mexico some time. "Down there if they don't like a call they come *after* you—with *tequila* bottles. I'm not shittin' ya. Unbelievable."

He nods, agreeing.

"This is a day at the beach," I tell him. "This is a walk in the—"

"You like Mexican food?" he asks.

"It's all right."

He starts telling me about a Mexican restaurant he goes to a lot.

"Hey, *Butter*," a player yells. "Got a full moon!"

"Do it, man," another says. "Go for it."

Hands in his pockets, Butter bends his knees a little, throws back his head, shuts his eyes and begins howling.

Everyone laughs, urging him on. And it *is* funny, this little roly-poly guy letting loose:

"*Ow-ow-owoooooo!*"

We're all laughing together.

* * *

Next inning I try being friendlier in the way I make my calls. Not so bossy.

"Well, that's a strike. Ju-u-ust caught the corner."

Or: "That's a ball. Close, but no cigar."

It doesn't work. The first questionable call, they're all over me again.

They seem to *despise* me.

When they don't agree with one of Butter's calls they say things like, "Aw, Butter, c'mon, man, *jeez*." When they don't like one of mine they tell me I'm worthless and pathetic.

They found out I'm not really the boss. That I'm not really anything at all. That I go from job to job to job. That I'm back with my parents now.

That next month I'll be thirty.

* * *

By the eighth inning every pitch looks like a strike and/or a ball. I try to be fair, this time calling it a strike, next time a ball.

I overhear the first baseman asking Butter, "Where'd you *get* this guy?"

I don't quite hear Butter's reply. Sounds like, "Mexico."

* * *

Then, in the top of the ninth, I call a strike on the lead-off batter and he actually bursts out laughing. He holds up his hand for "time" as he staggers out of the box, laughing and shaking his head.

That's it. I will not tolerate laughter. I whip off my mask and tell him, "You're outa the game!"

That stops him. "I'm *what*?" he says.

"Out of the game," I repeat. "Ejected. *Gone*." I point off the field for him to leave.

"What the hell *for*?"

"Unsportsmanlike laughter. Let's go."

"You're a *nutcase*. Hey, *Butter*."

"Never mind Butter. Off the field. Let's go. *Now*."

Butter comes trotting over. "What's up?"

"He's throwing me out for laughing. I can't laugh? What *is* this, *Russia*?

"My call," I tell Butter, in case he's thinking of interfering.

"That's right. Up to you," he says. "I don't know what you'll write in your *report*, but . . . "

"Outright and prolonged laughter intending to provoke," I tell him, as if quoting the Book.

Butter shrugs. "So toss him."

"*Butter!*"

"His call, Eddie."

I decide to be lenient and give this "Eddie" a warning. I point my finger at him: "No more laughter. Not a snicker." I slam on my mask. "Let's go. Play ball."

Butter trots back and Eddie steps into the batter's box again.

As the pitcher is peering in for the catcher's sign, I notice Eddie's bat begin vibrating. I look at him and he's trembling all over in the effort to keep from laughing. The pitcher, amused by this, steps off the rubber and stands there chuckling softly. The catcher sits back on his heels, giggling along.

Then Eddie finally lets go, reeling out of the box, dragging his bat, laughing loud and high. The fielders all join in. I look over at Butter and he turns away, his shoulders working.

I walk off the field.

*   *   *

Driving home, I still have all my gear on, even the mask.

Zen Buddhist Trainee

This cat keeps staring at me.

I'm sitting in the little lounge area of the crowded dining hall. We've got about five minutes before lunch and I'm trying to read an article in one of the Buddhist magazines on the coffee table. It's an interesting piece about the environmental cost of a single McDonald's hamburger. But this cat. He's sitting on the arm of the chair, inches away, staring at me.

I finally stop reading and look at him: *What's your problem?*

He continues staring.

I've seen him around. He's black and white and skinny and has some Japanese name, Tojo or Mojo or something. I've heard he's diabetic. They give him pills for it. The other day I walked into the lounge and about a dozen people were gathered around watching something taking place on the couch. Turned out to be Ryushin, one of the senior monks, trying to give the cat his pill. When he finally succeeded, everyone seemed so glad about it. In fact, not just glad but *happy.*

I'd like to be that way, you know? Happy because the cat took his pill.

Maybe that's why he's staring at me so hard. He's wondering, *What's someone like you doing in a nice place like this?*

I pat the top of his head to show him he's wrong about me. He cringes at my touch. I shove him off the chair and finish reading my article.

* * *

Richard the cook—the *tenzo*—strikes a stone bell and everyone shuts up and stands facing the little altar near the kitchen entrance. He lights some incense and we all do some chants together. Or they do. I have to get these chants down. Nothing makes you feel more alone than a bunch of people all chanting and you're not.

Richard carefully lights a candle.

He's a middleaged guy from Australia, scruffy and spaced-out-looking, but his kitchen is extremely clean and organized and he's a very good cook. It's all Buddhist-type food: lots of rice and vegetable dishes, lots of good soup, salads. I don't miss the meat at all. And after that article about McDonald's, forget it. No meat. Maybe an occasional cat.

I worked for Richard one afternoon, along with his assistant, a gigantic baldheaded softspoken monk named Gido (all the monks arc bald and have Jap names), the three of us in the big clean kitchen, pots and pans and ladles hanging from the ceiling over the big wooden cutting table, all sorts of good smells, and it was raining out. How nice that was.

I wore a gray apron and washed and cut carrots with an extremely sharp little Japanese hatchet. The carrots were these stubby little jobs from the monastery garden, the very carrots I had pulled from the ground only the day before while working with the baldheaded old-lady gardener-monk named Hojin—pulled them from the ground and brought them here and now I was cutting them up for everyone's lunch. So that was a good feeling.

Another good thing: there were enough carrots to keep me at it for a solid stretch and I could therefore work on trying to do my task with full Zen awareness. So whenever I found myself thinking something like, *Get a load of me in an apron slicing carrots in the kitchen of a Zen Buddhist monastery in the middle of the Catskill Mountains,* I would gently but firmly return my mind to the slicing of carrots . . . to the slicing of this particular carrot . . . to this particular slice.

As it turned out though, I had misunderstood Richard's instructions concerning how they should be cut. Not to make excuses, but he's got this Australian accent. Anyway, he wanted them in strips and I was chopping them into discs. But I didn't find out until I was all through. Meanwhile, chopping away, the rain on the roof, I felt a quiet happiness, even a certain serenity. Very unusual for me.

When I showed Richard all the chopping I had done, he shook his head. I thought he was showing amazement at how many, how quickly. But he said, "See, actually, what I wanted? I wanted 'em in strips."

"Oh," I said, all my quiet serene happiness shot to hell. *I can't do anything right!*

"Never mind," he said. "We'll use 'em like this."

"I'm really sorry."

"Not to worry, mate."

And his assistant Gido, the giant quiet monk, just to make me feel even worse, patted me on the shoulder as he walked by.

*　*　*

Today we're having some kind of tofu and vegetable dish with miso soup and dark heavy bread. I find a place at a long table with about ten people, all focusing on the guy to my immediate right, an esteemed guest from Hong Kong who's here to conduct a calligraphy workshop over the coming weekend. Which I don't think I'm going to attend. The trouble is, this guy looks a little too *much* like a Chinese master of calligraphy, in his black Zen pajamas and his long gray Chinese hermit's beard. And the way he speaks is right out of that TV show *Kung Fu*, with David Carradine as Kwai Chang Caine.

I used to watch that show a lot. There were always some completely unenlightened, greasy-looking cowboys about to gang up on Caine just because he was Chinese. And he would say to them very softly and quietly, with this look of totally sincere bewilderment:

"Why . . . do you wish . . . to harm me?"

And they'd say, "Cuz we don't like yer kind."

And Caine would ask them sincerely, "What . . . kind is that?"

And they'd say, "Chi-*nee*, that's what kind."

And only when he finally absolutely had to, when there just wasn't any other way out, would he go into Kung-Fu action, chopping and spinning and kicking, beating the hell out of all three or four of them with a mild look on his face, the whole scene taking place in slow motion, which I always took to represent the way Caine was seeing, with his absolute Zen concentration making everything go slow for *him* while continuing at regular speed for the bad guys, putting them at a serious disadvantage.

Anyway, this calligraphy fellow reminds me of Caine, the way he speaks. For example, just to be making conversation, since he's sitting right next to me and it would look bad if I didn't say *some*thing, I ask him if he experienced any jet lag after his flight from Hong Kong.

Right away I can feel everyone at the table rolling their eyes and thinking what a mundane question to ask such an esteemed personage.

"Jet . . . lag?" he says.

So now I have to explain about rapid travel through different time zones and the fatigue it can cause.

When I'm finally finished he says to me, "But . . . surely . . . we are always . . . here. Are we not?" And gives me an inscrutable little smile before returning to his bowl of tofu.

So now I'm supposed to sit here with my mind totally blown.

But you know what? I don't even think that's a real beard.
I'm serious.

*   *   *

I'm on lunch clean-up crew this week. Our crew chief is this
guy Allen who's a flaming gay, so I'm uneasy when he puts
his arm around my shoulder as he decides what to do with
me. "Let's see, why don't you . . . *I* know, why don't you go
out there with a tray and collect any bowls and utensils
naughty people haven't returned."

Back to being a busboy.

Out in the dining hall I come up to Hojin, the baldheaded
old-lady gardener-monk, sitting there telling some eager-look-
ing newcomer about her compost bins. He's listening as if
this is the most interesting thing he's heard in his life up to
now.

There's some empty bowls and utensils in front of them.

"Take this stuff?" I ask.

They look up.

"Oh, yes," she says.

And he says, "Sorry. We're s'pose to bring these back, I
know. I just . . ."

"Not to worry, mate," I tell him.

It goes well with everyone. No one treats me like a busboy. And then I get to the Chinaman, sitting there with his
empty bowl in front of him, speaking to the only other person at the table now, someone who wasn't there before, who's
sitting where I was sitting:

The Abbot.

He's a big lumberjack-looking guy, baldheaded of course, right now wearing an old faded flannel shirt, like anyone else. Except, he's not like anyone else. Not anyone *I* ever met, anyway.

My first experience of him was in the meditation hall—the *zendo*—as he was walking up and down the rows of us. As he passes, you're supposed to put your hands palm to palm, elbows out—in *gassho*—not only as a greeting but as a way of telling him you're awake and ready to go, ready to cut straight through to the core. But this guy on the cushion next to me was sitting there in the lotus position, hands cupped in his lap, softly snoring away.

"*Gassho*," one of the monitors called out to him as the Abbot approached, meaning get your palms together.

But he didn't hear. So the Abbot bent down as he passed and said in this not-very-loud but clear, clear voice:

"Wake up."

The guy woke up and put his hands in *gassho*.

I felt like *I* woke up too, all the thoughts in my head flying off like startled birds, and for a good half-minute my mind was as clear as the Abbot's voice.

I still hadn't actually seen him though, only his large bare feet as they passed. But I saw him shortly after that, in private.

It's called *dokusan*: a one-on-one interview with the Abbot. You go in this room just outside the meditation hall—the Dharma Room—and tell him about some problem in your practice, some wall you're up against, and he gives you advice. I hadn't prepared anything to say because I didn't know I'd be going that morning. I was sitting on my mat in the meditation hall with everyone else, breathing away, when suddenly one of the monks announced, "The *dokusan* line is open to those nearest the wall on the south side of the *zendo*." I don't know north from south but everyone in my row immediately got to their feet and *ran*—I'm serious—towards the back of the hall and knelt in a line outside his door. So I got up and trotted over.

By the time it was finally my turn I'd thought of a question for him, a good one. I wanted him to see that I may be just a lay trainee staying here for only a month but I'm still pretty deep. Here's what I would ask him:

"Abbot, how can one *strive* to attain enlightenment? Doesn't enlightenment require one to *relinquish* all striving?"

See how he handled *that* one.

When I heard the *ching* of his handbell I stood and walked eagerly to the door and entered. He was sitting on a mat on the other side of a bare wooden floor, in a black robe, eyes lowered, clutching his short polished Dharma stick in both fists across his lap.

I carefully closed the door, walked over and knelt before him. I began, as I'd been instructed, by telling him my first name and that my practice was counting-the-breath. Then, just as I was about to deliver my devastating question, he lifted his eyes and looked at me.

What can I tell you? He looked straight into my soul.

I know that sounds corny but that's what he did. He looked at me and there was nowhere to hide. I opened my mouth to speak, and all I could say was, "I'm sorry."

Tears ran down my face. I said it again, "I'm sorry."

Sorry for coming in here with a bullshit question designed to impress, sorry for all the bullshit that up to now had characterized my entire goddam life.

I wasn't apologizing to him or to Buddha, Jesus or God, my parents or anyone. I was just sorry.

And he understood. He didn't say anything, only nodded, but I could see—*any* fool could see—that he completely understood.

He lifted his bell and shook it, once. We bowed to one another. I got up and left.

Back in the *zendo*, on my mat, the tears kept coming. And then my nose started running. But we're not allowed to blow our nose or even sniff during meditation. We can sneeze or cough, since that's involuntary, but if your nose is running, let it run. Who cares? Nobody sees. Even so, it's a very unpleasant feeling, so I got all involved with ignoring my runny nose, and quit weeping for my sins.

* * *

Anyway, I come up with my tray to the table where the Abbot and the Chinaman are talking together quietly. The Chinaman is sitting up straight with his hands in his lap, the Abbot tilting back in his chair, hands behind his head, looking up as I approach.

I'm embarrassed: Yes, it's me, the weepy guy.

He nods pleasantly. I don't think he remembers me.

That hurts a little.

I ask the Chinaman if I can take his bowl and chop-sticks, and he'd better not try to show me up in front of the Abbot with some smartass inscrutable remark or I swear to God I'll grab that made-in-Hong Kong beard and yank it off his smug-looking face.

He says, "Oh. Yes. Please. Thank you."

Please and thank you. And then as I'm setting his bowl and chopsticks on my tray, he says to the Abbot, "He told me, he . . . *explained* to me, jet . . ." He looks at me, troubled. "What is the term?"

"Lag. Jet lag."

"*Yes*. Jet lag. *Thank* you," he says, and smiles at me with his crooked brown teeth.

And I smile at him.

And the Abbot smiles at both of us.

Moving on with my tray, I'm still not sure about the beard. I'm not sure about anything. This place is going to drive me around the bend. I'm sure about *that*.

Writer

1979–PRESENT

I didn't go crazy at the monastery. But I didn't attain enlightenment either. Didn't even come close. And when my month was up I drove away feeling deeply discouraged. I had counted on attaining enlightenment. Then I wouldn't have to worry any more about being a success or a failure. Imagine Buddha worrying about such a thing.

I drove around in the Catskill Mountains. It was beautiful there, especially now in the fall, but I wasn't looking, I was staring straight ahead. I drove around for hours. I'm not exactly sure what I was trying to do. Just get lost, I guess. So lost I would disappear or something.

I did get lost. And by then I was getting low on gas, the sun was going down—*was* down whenever the road would dip a little—and I started thinking about bears. I didn't want to run out of gas in the dark with bears around. I felt pretty certain about that.

I began looking for somewhere to stop and ask directions to the nearest town. But there wasn't anything on either side of the road except woods—deep dark woods, where the bears lived.

I finally came on a big open barn near the road and pulled off and got out. There was an old stone house atop a hill on the other side of the road. I walked up to the barn. A handwritten cardboard sign hung over the entrance: *Anteque Sale.* It was very dim in there.

"Don't be scared."

I whipped around.

A fat middleaged woman with high hair and a lot of makeup, in a ratty fur coat and gold slippers, walked up holding a kerosene lamp.

"Let there be light," she said, stepping past me into the barn, where she set the lamp down on the dirt floor. Then she turned around and spread her arms, indicating her wares: boxes of paperbacks, piles of old clothes, photo albums, plastic dolls, dirty vases, a stack of record albums, some rusty tools, an ironing board with a typewriter and toaster on it . . .

"Browse around," she told me. "And if you have any questions—"

"Actually, I just stopped to ask for directions."

She looked crushed. "Please buy something?" she asked. "All my friends are coming over for my birthday tomorrow and I can't even afford a new dress. You look like a nice man. Are you visiting? I noticed your plates. I've never been to Illinois. I've never been anywhere. But you don't want to hear my troubles. You want to look around. Do you enjoy the Tijuana Brass? I have all their records. They belonged to my husband. He would kill me if he knew. He went out to get a pack of cigarettes nine years ago and hasn't come back. Maybe he stopped off somewhere. Please buy something? All my friends are coming over." She was going to start crying.

I told her I would definitely buy something.

"You're a very kind person. What's your name? Mine's Dolores. Where did you say you were staying?"

"Well, I *was* staying at a monastery, a Zen—"

"A *monastery*. What happened? Don't tell me you gave up God for a woman. Please don't tell me *that* old story."

"No, I was just . . . basically visiting."

"Did you find peace there?"

"Well . . . "

"Sometimes I pray and that's what I ask for: peace of mind. 'Dear Lord,'" she prayed, folding her hands and closing her eyes, "'please bring me peace of mind. Please don't let me go crazy.'" She opened her eyes. "I want to show you something I think you'll appreciate, being a Catholic."

She went over to a shaky-looking card table covered with small items and returned with a little plastic Virgin Mary. "Isn't she cute?" She held it up to my face and tilted it side to side, speaking in a tiny voice: "Hi. My name is Mary. Won't you take me home with you? Please? I've never been to Illinois. Pleeease?"

"How much."

"One dollar. No, let's say three."

I pulled out my wallet and gave her three dollars, which she shoved in her coat pocket along with Mary.

I said to her, "The reason I stopped, I was wondering if you could direct me to the nearest—"

"Are you in some kind of trouble?"

"No, I'm just looking for—"

"Because I'm not about to help you escape from the police, if that's what you're thinking. You can stay here if you like, but I'm telling you right now, if the police come by wanting to know if I've seen a young—"

"I'm not in trouble, ma'am. I'm just trying to get to the nearest town. Really."

"Don't call me 'ma'am' like that. My name's Dolores, for God sakes."

"Dolores. Right. Sorry."

"Well, don't just stand there, look around. Help yourself. Anything you want, anything at all, you name it. That's what I'm here for. Then we'll talk about hideouts and God knows what. Go on, browse around. Please? Don't make me beg. Don't make me cry."

I knew I couldn't handle that, so I looked around, feeling very self-conscious with her standing there watching me.

"Both of those dolls are antiques," she said. "They're a pair. They belonged to my grandmother, who got them from *her* grandmother."

"Really?"

They were Barbie and Ken, both naked.

"Yes, 'really,'" she said, a little pissed off.

I moved on to a stack of photo albums. When I started opening one she said, "Please do not look through those

unless you're willing to buy. Those are very personal photo-
graphs and some of them are rather shocking. Not for the
faint of heart, I'm afraid. Twenty-five dollars for the whole
set."

I moved on.

"Those books are very old and rare," she said.

I looked through the box. They were paperback Harle-
quin Romances.

"Most of those authors you've probably never even heard
of," she added. "Twenty dollars for the entire box."

I nodded and moved on.

"The Tijuana Brass is planning a comeback," she said.
"Did you read about that? Those are their actual original
albums. Very hard to find. There's also some Hawaiian music
in there. Do you like Hawaiian music? My husband was
crazy about it. That's probably where he is right now, doing
the hula with some slut in a grass skirt. I'm sorry. It's none
of your business."

"That's all right."

"No, it is *not* all right."

I moved on to the ironing board, with a small typewriter
and toaster on it. There was a blank sheet of paper in the
typewriter and I tapped out a sentence I remembered from
typing class.

She came up beside me and read it out loud:

"'The quick brown fox jumps over the lazy dog.'"

She looked at me. "What a vivid description. Are you a
writer? I could *tell*. The moment I saw you I thought to

myself, *He's either a serial killer or some kind of writer.*
Imagine my relief!"

"Actually—"

"So what do you write, nature books? I prefer fiction
myself. I've read every one of those books you see over there,
every single one, and I'll tell you something, those people
are as real to me as—well, as *you* are. *More* real, since I
don't know anything about you, except that you're a writer,
which I think is wonderful. Let's say . . . ten dollars."

"Pardon?"

"Ten. For the typewriter."

"I don't really need one."

"What kind of writer doesn't need a typewriter?"

"I'm not a writer."

"Nonsense. Of course you are."

"No, really. I'm not."

"Then . . . " She brought her hand to her mouth.

"And I'm not a serial killer either. Honest to God,
ma'am."

"Dolores. The name's *Dolores.* Is that asking so much?"

"I'm sorry. I'm not a serial killer, Dolores."

"So what the hell *are* you then?"

I considered the question.

"I have no idea," I told her, and laughed. It seemed won-
derfully funny somehow. "Not a clue!" I said, and laughed
some more.

"Please don't laugh in front of me like that."

"I'm sorry," I said, then burst out laughing again. I
needed to sit down. I found a stool.

"Mind telling me what's so damn funny?"

I wiped my eyes. "Nothing. It's just . . . I don't know. I'm sorry."

"Comfortable?"

"Pardon?"

"Is that stool comfortable?"

"How much."

"Fifteen."

I got off it. "I should be going," I told her. "So could you tell me how to get to the nearest—"

"At least buy the *typewriter*, for God sakes. You have a gift. Don't waste it." She again read out loud, this time with feeling: "'The quick . . . brown fox . . . jumps over . . . the lazy . . . dog.' I can see that so clearly," she said, closing her eyes. "See that quick little fox. See that lazy, lazy dog."

"Ten, you said?"

"Fifteen, with the stool."

"I don't need a stool."

"All right, fifteen without the stool."

"Deal." I gave her a ten and a five. "That's all I can spend," I told her. "I need the rest to get home."

"Dear old Illinois. Is it nice there? People say how pretty it is out here in the mountains, but how would *I* know? I've never been anywhere else. And now all my friends are coming over and I have nothing to wear. If I just had two more dollars . . . "

"Here. Buy a nice dress."

"What for?" she said, pocketing the bills. "So I can sit there looking beautiful all by myself?"

"What about—"

"My friends? What friends? I haven't got any friends. Are you kidding? You think if I had any friends I'd be out here talking to *you*? Try to be serious. No offense but I wouldn't sleep with you if you were the last man on the planet." She shook her head. "Stick to nature writing, fella. Because I'll tell you something. Just between you and me? You don't know much about the real world. And you sure don't know much about *women*."

I nodded, agreeing.

"I have to be going now," I told her, and once again asked directions to the nearest town.

She said there was one about a mile and a half up the road.

"You're kidding."

"I think I should know."

I lifted the typewriter. "Well, Dolores . . . "

"*Take me with you, take me with you*," she said in a tiny voice, holding out the plastic Mary. She put it in my coat pocket and patted the place.

We walked together out to my car.

"Would you do something for me?" she asked.

"If it's money, I'm sorry but I really—"

"In one of the books you write? Even if it's only about animals? Would you mention me? Just . . . say that I was here. That Dolores Van Buren was here. That you met me and . . . say that she had a lovely smile. 'Dolores had a lovely smile.' Would you say that in your book?"

I promised her I would.

We were at the car. She looked around at the sky, her arms folded closely. "Getting dark earlier and earlier," she said quietly, and sighed. "How I hate that."

I told her I understood.

She stepped closer. "You can kiss me, if you like, just here," offering her cheek. "That's it. Thank you. Whoops, now you've got powder on your mouth. Something to remember me by."

I didn't wipe it off. "Goodbye," I said to her.

"Goodbye," she said, and smiled.

Dolores had a lovely smile.